Zero the Slaver: Monster of Cruelty

An Adventure in Equatorial Africa

LAWRENCE FLETCHER

Table of Contents

Chapter 1: Missing..5

Chapter 2: A Night of Horror.. 12

Chapter 3: Black Ivory... 16

Chapter 4: The Mouth of Hell 23

Chapter 5: The Secret of The Pass...................................... 27

Chapter 6: Richard Grenville, His Mark 30

Chapter 7: Just in Time 39

Chapter 8: Zero 49

Chapter 9: The War Trail... 55

Chapter 10: No Quarter.. 60

Chapter 11: The People of The Stick 66

Chapter 12: Fighting the Flames.. 70

Chapter 13: In Freedom's Cause 76

Chapter 14: Equatoria 81

Chapter 15: Hope... 86

Chapter 16: Alive from the Dead 90

Chapter 17: Quod Dixi Dixi 97

Chapter 18: A Friend in Need 103

Chapter 19: A Forced March... 107

Chapter 20: The Hand of God 112

Chapter 21: Lost and Found 117

Chapter 22: Farewell.. 122

Chapter 1: Missing

1,000 Pound Reward

The above-named Sum will be paid to any person giving information which will lead to the discovery of the whereabouts of a young Englishman named Richard Grenville, who was last seen at Durban on 15th December, 1877.

Apply to Masterton and Driffield, Advocates, Port Natal.

Facing this striking announcement, and with his back to the Standard Bank of South Africa, in Durban, stood, one morning in July, 1880, a wiry-looking, clean-shaved man of about five- or six-and-thirty, dressed in a rough grey homespun suit.

Man after man paused, read, marked, learned, and, no doubt, inwardly digested, the contents of the advertisement, then passed on his way without giving the matter a second thought--beyond, perhaps, half wishing, in a lazy sort of way, that he knew something about this man who seemingly was so much wanted by his own people. But our grey-coated friend still stood there, and appeared to be literally devouring the announcement.

At length he turned sharply away with a muttered "Hum! It's a big pile. Five thousand dollars--now, I wonder if--" But here his keen eye noted the stoppage of another person--a fashionably-dressed man--before the advertisement, which seemed of considerable personal interest to him, judging from the way he stared at it, and from the fact that his cigar dropped from his lips, which mechanically opened with an involuntary exclamation the moment the wording caught his eye. Quickly recovering himself, the man glanced keenly at grey-coat, who was, however, diligently charging his pipe, and then he, too, like his predecessors, passed on his way.

"Snakes!" muttered our friend. "Now, I wonder who that swell is, and why this lay startled him so infernally. Reckon I'll have to get you weighed up before I clear, old chap;" and, lighting his pipe, he moved briskly away in the direction of Masterton and Driffield's office.

Arrived there, he in due course expressed to a young clerk his desire to interview one of the principals on the subject of a considerable interest which he proposed to acquire in certain land at Durban, and very shortly found himself closeted with Mr. Driffield.

"I have called, sir," he said, "to see you regarding this advertisement of yours for one Richard Grenville, and to learn what further details you can afford me beyond the information given in the announcement."

Our friend, be it observed, was something of a curiosity. A thorough-bred Yankee, he seldom or never indulged in "Americanisms" of any kind except when soliloquising, which he had a singular habit of doing whilst deducing his own peculiar theories.

"Oh!" said the lawyer, in a somewhat aggrieved tone. "My clerk stated that you wished to consult me with regard to the purchase of some land. That advertisement was only printed off last night, and if we have had one call concerning it, we have already had at least two hundred."

"I didn't choose to let your clerk know my business, or anything about me, Mr. Driffield," replied grey-coat curtly; "but here's my card, sir, and now let me hear all you've got to say, without further loss of time."

Mr. Driffield took the pasteboard, read it, and stared blankly at the other, who laughed quietly, and then reached out his hand, which the lawyer grasped in most unmistakably hearty fashion.

"Why, God bless me, Kenyon," said he, "I should never have known you in this get-up; but look here, come and dine with me to-night, and we'll go right into this business. You are the one man I would have chosen for it out of all the world, and I shall be very much mistaken if I haven't a good twelve months' work for you. To-night, at seven, at the Athenaeum, then. And now good morning,' for I'm up to the eyes in work. Oh! by the way, Kenyon, if you haven't read this book, do so at once, there's a good fellow, for it contains a full account of Grenville's South African adventures, and your perusal of it will prepare my way, and save me going over most of the old ground again to-night." So saying, the lawyer dismissed his visitor, who was none other than Stanforth Kenyon, the keenest and wiliest detective New York could boast of--a man born to his profession, and consequently an ornament to it.

At five-and-twenty Kenyon was an unknown, but--having regard to his literary merit--an overpaid scribbler on one of the big New York dailies; but now, only ten years later, he was universally admitted to be the most unerring sleuth-hound of the whole shrewd band of secret police owning allegiance to Uncle Sam, and whose business in South Africa at the present time, needless to say, was known only to himself.

At once retaking his way to the hotel he had left that morning, the detective settled down to read the book in question, ["Into the Unknown"] and in a few hours' time had mastered its contents, and lay quietly back in his chair, smoking, and thinking deeply.

After a further hour had been expended in this comforting and, no doubt, edifying fashion, he took out a well-worn notebook, and wrote several lines therein in shorthand; then, returning the book to his pocket, he started out for a stroll, and seven o'clock saw him seated opposite to the lawyer, and enjoying most thoroughly the excellent dinner provided for him by that worthy gentleman.

"And now," said Mr. Driffield, when the cloth was removed and both men had lighted their cigars, "let me have your opinion of `Into the Unknown,' or, rather, as to what extent the events narrated therein may or may not bear upon the present disappearance of our friend Grenville."

"First," said the detective, calmly begging the question, and taking out his notebook, "who are you working for, Mr. Driffield? I mean," he added, quickly, "is it some relation of Grenville's who is anxious about the missing man, or have you yourself any personal interest in the search?"

"None at all," was the reply. "Let me be quite frank with you, Kenyon. I am employed by his cousin, Lord Drelincourt, who shared his adventures amongst the Mormons, and my lord is in no end of a taking about him. You see, the two men were like twin brothers all their lives, and now that Lord Drelincourt has lost his wife and child, he feels alone in life, poor fellow, and would give his whole fortune to have his cousin by his side."

"How very sad," commented the detective. "So he took poor Dora Winfield homo only to bury her. How did it all happen?"

"No one knows," said the little lawyer, dropping his voice. "Poor Lady Drelincourt and her one-year-old boy were found dead in bed one morning, without even the suspicion of a mark of violence upon them.

"My lord was away from home when it happened, and the shock almost unseated his reason, and for weeks after the sad event he was down with brain fever. Though quite a young man, his hair turned snowy-white when he realised the awful extent of his cruel loss, and awoke from his long illness only to find that his dead had long been buried out of his sight. Doctors and detectives were called in at the time, but everything was in vain. The detectives were hopelessly at fault, and the only theory the doctors could advance was that mother and child had been chloroformed to death.

"The servants were old family retainers, and were entirely beyond suspicion, being all of them passionately devoted to their sweet young mistress, and bound to their loved master as much by his personal worth and goodness as by the unbroken ties of voluntary servitude during three generations.

"And now, Kenyon, will you undertake the case? The reward is already well worth working for, great though the risks may be; but I can undertake to double it if you bring our man in alive. You will get a fine sporting holiday up country, with all expenses liberally provided for, and in point of fact it is the opportunity of a lifetime--or perhaps I ought to say that to anyone but yourself it would be such."

The detective sat thinking for awhile, and then said, "See here, Mr. Driffield; this is a large order--a very large order--and I must just reason the matter out in my own way; but I'll let you have my answer by or before this time to-morrow. Your man may be only shooting in the far interior, or camping out in this infernal secret territory of the Mormons, or he may be--well, elsewhere."

The two then separated for the night, the lawyer going straight to the telegraph station, and in a few minutes more the submarine cable had the following message flashing over it:--

"To Drelincourt, London.

"Splendid man probably available; terms, two thousand and expenses. Shall I secure him?

"Driffield."

Arrived at his hotel, the detective sought his own room, lighted his pipe, and puzzled over his notebook for upwards of an hour, idly drumming on the table with his fingers, and listlessly turning over the leaves pregnant with flotsam and jetsam of criminal interest, and glancing from time to time in a half-attentive, half-indifferent fashion at a number of pencilled faces which adorned its earlier pages. Suddenly, however, his attention became riveted, the man's face seemed as if turned to stone and his whole expression transformed whilst he gazed fixedly at one portrait as if unable to believe his eyes.

"Gods!" he cried at last, springing excitedly to his feet; "I have it! Aha! Master Zero, we shall meet at last, and then look out for yourself, my friend, for if ever I entertained hatred and malice and all uncharitableness, it is towards you, and with good cause; and, Heaven helping me, before next year is out, I'll pay you back a little of the debt, the fearful debt, I owe you."

8

Quickly he also proceeded to the cable offices, and a few minutes later another message--this time in cypher--traversed the ocean depths, as follows:--

"To Heliostat, New York.

"Kingdom rage offing."

Which being interpreted meant--

"To the Chief of Police, New York.

"Wire latest information Zero's movements."

Early next morning the cable company handed out two messages, first to--

"Driffield. Port Natal.

"Secure at any cost. Wire result."

Second to--

"Wilkinson, Alexandra Hotel, Durban.

"Noughts and crosses hades horrify handfast holy ostrich."

Meaning--

"Sailed for England 15th April, 1879; left France for Madagascar about September same year."

Eagerly seizing his message, the detective hurriedly mastered its contents, and with an emphatic grunt of satisfaction started off instantly for the lawyer's office, and an hour later yet another message was flashed across the seas--

"To Drelincourt, London.

"Secured; starts immediately."

To which Mr. Driffield was considerably astonished to receive the prompt reply--

"To Driffield, Port Natal.

"Let him wait my arrival. Sail Tartar to-morrow, bringing all needful equipment.--Drelincourt."

His lordship arrived in due course, and the lawyer was inexpressibly shocked at the change which had taken place in the appearance of his client. The man looked twenty years older, but was nevertheless strong, vigorous, and stern, and the detective noted with secret joy the hard-set lines in his patron's face, and felt that here at least there would be no faltering or shrinking, no quarter given and none required, when the bitter end came; for bitter did this astute man-hunter already feel certain that the end would prove to be.

The two men were fast friends in a very short time, and one of his lordship's earliest instructions to Kenyon and the lawyer was to conceal his identity as far as possible by addressing him simply under his family name of Leigh, by which he had been known when a younger son, and, in all human probability, the reverse of likely to become a peer of the realm.

Months later, Leigh and Kenyon, with their full complement of native bearers, bade a long farewell to the shores of the mighty lake of Victoria Nyanza, and struck out boldly into central Africa, steering hard and fast by the equatorial line.

Leigh, as we shall continue to call Lord Drelincourt, was naturally curious to know why the detective, who held the compass and took all the observations, should be so extremely particular about his latitude, but that worthy either could or would give no explanation, and Leigh had already acquired such implicit confidence in every action of his self-constituted guide, that he let himself be led blindly whithersoever the American chose to take him, feeling that the man was either working confidently upon "information received," or that his faculty of instinct was so finely developed that he was unlikely to make any very serious mistakes.

As a matter of fact Leigh was right to a certain extent, for starting with a theory of his own, which had the rooted belief of Zero's complicity in the disappearance of Grenville for its point of departure, the American, whilst waiting the arrival of his patron from England, had worked up several slender clues, and had afterwards elaborated them in a manner calculated to have made his yet far-distant foe feel the reverse of comfortable, had he been conscious of the very tender interest taken by an outsider in the most trifling actions performed by him during the past, both distant and relatively near.

By careful watching, and by shadowing in a variety of inimitable disguises, Kenyon, who was an infinitely better actor than many a man who makes his living "on the boards," had soon unearthed, become intimate with, and pretty well "weighed up"--to use his own expression-- the gentleman who had exhibited such unequivocal signs of dismay when unexpectedly confronted with the advertisement concerning Grenville, and the detective had satisfied himself that this fellow, Crewdson Walworth by name, was a man with a history, could he but find it out--a history, moreover, which instinct assured him would prove to be of the greatest service to the Grenville search party at the present juncture. More, he also knew for a fact that his friend Crewdson corresponded in cypher with someone at Zanzibar, but even the cunning of Stanforth Kenyon had totally failed to ascertain who that someone was, or by what name he or she was designated, or, indeed, to get out of Master Crewdson Walworth anything else at all worth knowing.

The detective, however, had put two and two together, and had built up a theory in his usual cautious fashion, and every step of the ladder, though most rigidly and thoroughly tested, had thus far proved to be absolutely correct, and his deductions to be altogether justified by the course of events.

Chapter 2: A Night of Horror

No serious mishap befell our pair of adventurers until they neared the Katonga River, but just here they dropped in for a streak of ill-luck, which was like to have brought the expedition to a premature and utterly disastrous termination.

Leaving their men in camp one morning, Leigh and Kenyon had set out to thoroughly and carefully explore a mighty kloof, or gorge, in the adjacent hills, expecting to complete their investigations easily in a couple of hours or thereabouts.

As the pair entered this natural mountain fastness, however, it rapidly developed into a deep gorge, along which trickled a stream of water so tiny that it frequently lost itself altogether amongst the stones which served it for a bed.

On either hand great grey barren walls shot up like precipices, whilst mighty scarped-out rocks seemed to hang over the very heads of the explorers, the giant walls elsewhere being thickly fringed towards the skyline with trees and bushes, many of the former absolutely hanging head-downwards, and appearing to maintain their precarious tenure of existence solely by the aid of magnificent festoons of creepers, which hung from tree to rock, and from rock to tree, these gigantic parasites absolutely sustaining the decayed trunks of many a long-dead monarch of the woods, which they had enfolded in their tenacious and eventually fatal embrace; higher still the foliage upon the very summit of the cliffs looked like narrow gleaming threads of green and gold against the dull background of soft sandstone rock. Within the kloof it was unquestionably more or less dark at the best of times, but just now darker than usual, for a vast white cloud, which the pair had noticed in the distance when they entered the pass some hours before, had gradually and ominously settled down, until it seemed to hang like a veritable curtain of rich, fleecy wool directly over the chasm; and as our friends were in the act of discussing the advisability of taking the back track to camp, and returning to complete their investigations on the morrow, this cloud suddenly burst over their very heads, and in one short moment transformed their rocky road into an angry, swelling torrent of leaden-coloured water, alive with branches, trees, and stones, and this now rushed foaming and roaring down the awful pass, sweeping everything before it, and threatening each instant to engulf the two wretched men, who had saved themselves for the nonce by hanging on to a tree trunk which was jammed cross-wise in the narrow gully of rock.

Suddenly Leigh gave a gasp, turned white as death, and relaxed his hold, but ere the water could sweep him away he was in the iron grasp of the American; many an enemy had known to his bitter cost what it was to feel the clutch of the detective, but never had that grip of steel stood a friend in so good a stead as now.

A floating log had struck Leigh violently on the side, dislocating a rib and causing him to swoon away. For several anxious moments it seemed to Kenyon that one or both of them must go, but to his intense relief he suddenly noticed that the rush of the water was becoming less swift, and Leigh at the same time pulling round again to some extent, the twain were soon in comparative safety from the water, which vanished almost as rapidly as it had appeared.

By this time, however, evening was coming on, and this, in the depths tenanted by our friends, quickly meant the darkness of Erebus, and unpleasant though it was, they had no alternative but to sit patiently on their friendly log and wish for daylight. The unfortunates had not even the consolation of a smoke, for both tobacco and matches had been reduced to a mere pulp by the water, nor had they aught in the shape of food or drink save a handful of unpleasantly damp peppermints owned by the American, and a pint of good brown brandy in Leigh's flask.

Now most people will concede that under such circumstances the consumption of the brandy was not only permissible but distinctly advisable, though very few, perhaps, would care to tackle the peppermints.

Not so, however, our friends, for not once nor twice had they been indebted at a pinch entirely to these simple "sweets" for keeping body and soul together during long days and anxious nights, when, with savage foes following keen-eyed and red-handed on their tracks, any stoppage for food or fire would have meant certain sudden death.

All that Kingsley has said regarding the use of the "divine weed" may be re-written, and with much more truth, in favour of the harmless and not more odorously objectionable peppermint. "A lone man's companion, a hungry man's food, a sad man's cordial, a chilly man's fire;" all this, and more, did the despised peppermint prove to our friends that awful night, and needless to say they appreciated their oft-tried food at its honest value. Under the coldest conditions it

13

was acceptable to a degree, and almost equally so under a blazing sun, with the thermometer registering 80 degrees in the shade, for whilst it comforted the inside of the body, it cooled the fevered palate by causing every breath of burning tropic air to rush into the mouth like draughts of nectar, laden with a welcome icy message from the far unlovely north.

Slowly the hours passed away, so slowly that the American thought his companion would die of exposure, for he was still suffering keenly from the blow his side had received, and never was dawn more welcome to man than when those two miserable mortals at last saw it blushing golden upon the trees far above them, followed by the glorious sun glinting upon the damp metallic-looking rocks, till the whole angry chasm was bathed in a tremulous reddening glow of lovely light and shade.

A weary way it seemed back to camp; indeed, it is doubtful in the extreme if Leigh would ever have reached it, had the pair not been met half-way by their anxious sable retainers, who did not in the least degree appreciate the honour of being left in unsupported possession of this great lone land; these men very soon had their masters under canvas, and after a steaming cup of coffee, stowed them away inside their blankets and left them to the undisturbed enjoyment of their well-earned repose.

For several days Leigh was in a high fever, consequent upon the dislocated rib, but this having been carefully put to rights by the skilful Kenyon, he rapidly mended, and their camp being fortunately placed in a healthy position, he was completely recovered at the end of a few weeks, and again ready and eager to betake himself to the search for his cousin.

With returning health, Leigh had betrayed an increased desire to extract precise information from Kenyon as to the why and wherefore of their present position, but all the satisfaction he could obtain from that worthy was a laconic assurance that so far they had made no mistakes, and that at that moment they were either very near their destination, or else were on the tail-end of a trail which had been blinded with consummate skill Kenyon had, he himself said, been very far from idle during Leigh's illness, and had thoroughly exploited the district, and taken a number of photographs in the immediate vicinity; but he had come to the conclusion that nothing of practical utility could be accomplished until Leigh was fit to return with him to the pass and again take up the thread of search where they had dropped it, and he added that if naught of Richard Grenville was written on its silent walls, he would then be completely

14

nonplussed.

Kenyon, as Leigh had long since learned, was no ordinary police detective; he was a shrewd and skilful tracker, a man born and brought up on the frontier of the Far West, and his experience had been dearly bought in many an Indian fight and foray before he gravitated to New York to try his hand at journalism as favoured by the New World.

A crack shot with the revolver, and no mean exponent of the beauties of the Winchester repeater, he was at all times a man to be feared by his foes, and to be looked up to by his friends, as a veritable tower of strength.

Of Leigh we need say little, beyond remarking that he was in the prime of manhood, was as strong as a bull, and had lost none of his skill with the rifle, whilst he had derived a new, and to his enemies a doubly dangerous energy, begotten of his loves and of his hates; to him it seemed that, could they but find his cousin Dick, nothing would be impossible with such heads and hearts as Grenville and Kenyon possessed, especially if he were himself there to take a third hand at the game.

Chapter 3: Black Ivory

Having arranged to recommence their search at dawn of day, our friends turned in to rest that night, leaving one of their Zanzibaris on guard. This man had thus far shown himself fairly reliable, and being a very great coward, had proved a most excellent watchman, seldom failing to alarm the camp, at least once every night, with the fearsome news that bloodthirsty foes, in some shape or form, were close upon them, the attacking force, nine times out of ten, existing only in his fertile imagination, and turning out to be either hungry and inquisitive beasts of prey, or the grey mists of early dawn rising to greet the sun.

These constant scares had naturally had the effect of inclining everyone in the camp to cry "Wolf!" turn over in his blanket, and, after roundly anathematising the alarmist, to go comfortably to sleep again; but when Kenyon was roused by this man on the night in question, a single glance convinced him that the fellow was, at all events, in desperate earnest, for his knees knocked together, and his face was fairly grey with the horror of some new and unexplained phenomenon, as he stammered out his statement to the effect that several hundred men were silently creeping upon their position, under cover of the mist, and asserting that he could see them sufficiently clearly to count their numbers by the moonlight.

"Let my master," he said, "open his white eyes as clear as crystal, and see my tongue, for there is no lie upon it." Picking up his rifle, Kenyon roused Leigh, the pair quickly following the watchman outside the tent, and this was what they saw.

Slightly to their right, and entering ghost-like the suspected mountain gorge, was a long train of human beings moving silently, yet swiftly, westwards.

The camp was completely shrouded in mist, and altogether invisible to these people passing it within stone's-throw, but its occupants by lying down could see tolerably well beneath the thick grey curtain, which overhung them in every direction, and it did not require a second glance to satisfy the Europeans that the spectacle they were watching was simply an African slave caravan, of unusually large dimensions, on the march. For some minutes the pair gazed in silence, and then with a fierce but subdued ejaculation, Leigh endeavoured to spring to his feet, but was held still by the iron hand of the detective.

"Down, man. Down, for your life!" he whispered. "The game is only just beginning."

"But curse it all," growled Leigh, "don't you see that most of the slaves are white, and that many of them are women?"

"I see it all," was the answer, in a stern incisive whisper, "but I see little beyond what I expected to see when we arrived here a month ago. Just wait a while, and if I know anything of my work, these people will lead us to your cousin. If we follow them to their destination, there I am convinced shall we find Richard Grenville, if he be still in the land of the living."

For fully half an hour did the wretched troop continue to file past, and then captives, white and black, male and female, together with their countless guards, were engulfed in the eerie shadows of the rocky gorge, and entirely lost to human ken. Not a sound had the anxious watchers heard from first to last, and when the hindmost figure vanished from sight, Leigh could not refrain from rubbing his eyes to see if he were really awake and not dreaming; then, becoming satisfied that the former was the case, he seized his rifle, turned eagerly to Kenyon, and begged him to get on the trail of these nocturnal wanderers without another moment's delay.

Here, again, however, Leigh's fiery impetuosity was confronted by the stubborn coolness of the American, that worthy absolutely refusing to make any movement for at least another hour.

"No, thank you, Leigh," he said; "if yonder poor creatures are captives to the man who I firmly believe has them in his grip, all I say is just look out for squalls. You may take my word for it that before you got your foot inside the pass you would be simply riddled with bullets. I dare stake my reputation that there are not less than a score of scouts outlying all around us, and we have to thank this very substantial veil of mist for saving our lives, for the moment, at all events. In another hour the entire crowd will have got some way through the gorge, and then the scouts will draw in, and give us a chance of moving, but it would be sheer madness on our part to stir from our present position before dawn."

"Wherever can those blackguards possibly have laid hands on the dozens of white men and women we saw in the caravan?" asked Leigh.

"Ah! Now you are making a great mistake," replied Kenyon. "There were at most only half-a-dozen white men amongst the captives, and I saw but one white woman; the rest were unfortunate creatures from one of the native tribes south of

17

the Great Lakes, and whose habit it is to plaster their bodies with grey ashes. The first glance under this misty-looking moon deceived me, too, but I can reassure you on that score. There were, quite half-a-dozen white men amongst them, though, and as for the white woman, the less said about her the better, for she was one of the slave-drivers. I think, however, Leigh, that you are missing the main point offered to us in this affair. Don't you see that by all the laws of reason and common-sense this caravan should be steering due east for the seaboard, and here we find slaves obviously imported from a distance (for I never heard of the grey ash colouring being practised anywhere in this latitude) being driven due west. Now, if you will take your map for what it is worth, or will question any of these frauds of ours called Guides,' you will find that there is no town of any kind in this vicinity, nothing, indeed, of any note at all within hundreds of miles, so far as is known, let alone any such thing as a slave market. Whither, then, can this immense caravan possibly be going?

"Another point that impressed itself upon my notice was the fact that the slave-drive was composed entirely of full-grown men and women (it positively did not contain one single youth or child), all of which looks as if the strongest slaves had been purposely selected for severe labour of some kind in the interior, far or near, their ultimate destination and precise occupation being what we have to find out."

"Give me to understand your whole theory, Kenyon, and why you connect these people with my cousin," said Leigh.

"No!" was the curt reply. "I have no theory; at least, I have as yet only the very faintest suspicion of one, and the possibilities before us are far too vast for me at present to hazard even the remotest guess at either the final result of all this, or whither our investigations will ultimately lead us; only I believe, nay, I am morally certain, that in following yonder caravan--if follow it we can--we shall be treading in the steps taken voluntarily by the remnant of the Mormons who escaped from Grenville's vengeance in East Utah, and who were, I am equally sure, succeeded at a later date by your cousin, and probably by many of his Zulu friends, as part and parcel of just such a slave caravan as we have seen to-night. And now let us stop talking and get to work at some food, for the light is beginning to grow, and in half-an-hour's time we ought to be ready to move. I have slipped two of our fellows into the long grass with orders to keep their wits about them, but I expect the cowards will lie so close for the sake of their own precious skins that they will see nothing, however much there may be for them to observe."

"Ay!" said Leigh, bitterly, "I wish we had a handful of our old Zulu allies here and we would make it very warm for the slavers; but as for these wretched curs, they are not worth their salt, except to carry loads, which they will throw to the deuce at the veriest shadow of approaching danger."

As soon as the sun had fairly risen and sucked up the mist, the camp was struck, and the entire party entered the rocky defile and proceeded to thread its dark avenues with the utmost caution, all of which, however, seemed totally unnecessary, as they nowhere saw the slightest sign of life, or the remotest indication that the stony way had ever before been trodden by the foot of man.

One thing, nevertheless, struck the Europeans as being most singular, and this was the fact that when they had penetrated a very considerable way through the gorge, and arrived at the spot where Leigh's unfortunate accident had occurred, they discovered the roadway to be absolutely closed by the fallen tree which had so staunchly stood their friend on the occasion of their previous visit, and which was still firmly jammed endwise across the narrow rugged path.

This obstruction was very carefully examined, but it bore no traces of having been tampered with in any shape or form, nor was there the slightest mark upon it which would lead even the most suspicious to believe that the obstacle had been climbed over by either man or beast.

Kenyon at last decided that it would be best for them to mount the log and proceed on their way, arguing that if the people they sought were really concealed anywhere in the kloof--which certainly did not appear to offer even sufficient cover for a fox--they must be on the watch, and any attempt to return and investigate would be the signal for instant destruction, whilst if their party, on the other hand, passed quietly onwards, the slavers would probably conclude that it was composed of explorers and was best left alone, knowing what an awkward habit England has, during her spasms of activity, of beating up the world at large for her missing scientific men.

This course was accordingly adopted, on the principle of choosing the least of two evils, and before night fell, the party had left the dismal gorge behind them, and were sitting comfortably round their camp fire, after having taken the precaution to post two scouts near the exit of the kloof, with instructions that, should anything suspicious occur, one of them was instantly to come into camp with the news. All, however, remained perfectly quiet, and the night passed without an alarm of any kind, even the ultra-particular night-watchman failing for once to discover so much as the shadow of one of his customary nocturnal horrors.

Thus did Leigh and his astute comrade for the second time miss the secret of the place, or, as it is known amongst the scattered native tribes, the "Black Pass of the Dark Spirit of Evil."

For hours that evening did Leigh and Kenyon discuss the question of the mysterious disappearance of the slave caravan, for that those who composed it had not penetrated as far as their own present position they had quite satisfied themselves before pitching their tent for the night.

The outer, or western end of the rocky defile debouched upon highlands of soft spongy turf, and this nowhere bore the slightest impress of a human foot, which it would most certainly have done had anyone crossed it recently; indeed, had the "slave-drive" passed that way, the whole place would have been paddled like a sheep pen.

"You may well cudgel your brains, Leigh," said Kenyon, after hours of profitless arguing on the following night, "for those fellows never left the kloof either by this end or the other after they once entered it. Tell me, Leigh," he continued, venturing a question, which, hardened man-hunter that he was, had scores of times trembled upon the tip of his tongue in the past few months, and had yet remained unasked--"tell me, have you no clue, no idea, and absolutely no theory as to who was responsible for the murder of your wife and child? for foully murdered I am quite convinced they were."

Vitally important as the query was, Kenyon would have given all he possessed could he have withdrawn the words ere they were well spoken, for the fearful anguish depicted in the countenance of his friend gave him, for but one second as it were, a fleeting glimpse of the agony of soul in which this strong man lived from day-to-day, and from hour to hour. The misery of expression was awful, but a glance infinitely less keen than that of the skilled detective would have noted, with a wealth of pity, that it was a misery which had never learned to say "Thy will be done."

For full five minutes did Leigh hide his face in his hands and give no answering sign, and it was the detective who had once again to break the dread silence.

"Forgive me," he said, "old friend, if I have torn the quivering wound anew, and believe me when I say that not idle curiosity, but dire necessity, as I conceived it, on behalf of the living, could have made me touch upon the hallowed subject of the loved but unavenged dead." And he rose to walk away.

Quickly Leigh raised his face, lined, as it seemed to his friend, in one short five minutes with a whole lifetime of keenest suffering.

"Stop, Kenyon," he said hoarsely, "and excuse my want of self-control. You are right, the loved and unforgotten dead are passed from us for a season, peace be with them! Now let us see what we can do to pay our debts--an eye for an eye, a tooth for a tooth, ay, and blood for blood! See here," and he laughed a discordant laugh, which wrung Kenyon's very soul by the pitiful wail with which it closed, as the strong man broke down and sobbed in a bitter agony of keen remembrance. "See here," he said, as he again pulled himself together, and opened the back of his watch, from which he extracted a small scrap of paper, "they found this pinned to the coverlid of my darling's bed."

The detective reached over and took the paper, but before looking at it he poured out, and insisted upon Leigh drinking, a stiff glass of brandy, for he saw that his friend was completely unhinged.

This done, he turned his whole attention to the morsel of paper lying in his hand, and this was what he saw. Simply a small white sheet with a circular, dead black line drawn thus upon it:--

Pinned on a dead woman's breast, what did this senseless hieroglyphic mean?

To doctors and detectives, nothing!

To the bereaved and desperate husband, nothing!!

To Stanforth Kenyon, the wily American detective, nothing!!!

"Nothing!" gentle reader. Just that, and no more.

One glance he gave--but one; then, springing to his feet, fairly palpitating with excitement, he almost screamed, "I knew it. I knew it, Zero! Zero! by the Living God!" and as if it were a sombre echo of his words, a rifle spirted its vivid jet of flame from the outer gloom beyond the camp fire, and one of the native guides sitting just behind Kenyon sprang into the air with a bullet through his brain, and fell to the ground a corpse.

Instantly the whole party sought cover, but no further attempt of any kind was made to molest them, and when morning dawned they could nowhere find a trace of the dastard who had fired the fatal shot, and all that remained for them to do was to bury the body of their poor, unoffending servant, and choose out a safer camping ground where they might, perhaps, obtain immunity from such unpleasant nocturnal visitors.

Through the livelong night the thoughts of both Leigh and Kenyon had, as may well be imagined, been very busy; but whilst Leigh was entirely absorbed in the one idea of avenging his murdered wife and child, the purposes of the American went deeper. He, too, had a righteous act of retribution to perform, but he had also first, in the execution of his duty, to find Grenville alive, and release him, if it could be done; and then, again, vengeance, according to his idea, would not be consummated by a bullet wound or a spear-thrust: he simply yearned to get his hated enemy in his clutches, and to make him ignominiously expiate the countless crimes of his villainous life under the hands of the public executioner, but feared that such a triumph would be utterly unobtainable, for, setting aside all other considerations, and glancing at Leigh's stern, set countenance, Kenyon felt that the common enemy would receive but short shrift so far as the Englishman was concerned if once he fell into the power of the little band.

Clearly, however, it was little use as yet planning the cooking of a hare which appeared much more likely to catch them than to allow the reverse to happen, and until they knew how and where the enemy was posted it was absolutely necessary to exercise the greatest discretion, which, in vulgar parlance, meant "making themselves scarce," which they accordingly did without further loss of time, giving the place leg-bail, and putting five-and-twenty miles between themselves and the kloof ere they again halted for the night.

Chapter 4: The Mouth of Hell

Leigh had naturally asked Kenyon for an explanation of his wild excitement consequent upon the production of the treasured scrap of paper, and for information concerning the murderer whom he designated as "Zero," and these details the American had promised to give him the moment he was absolutely sure that the man whom he now knew to be, without a doubt, responsible for the deaths of Lady Drelincourt and her infant son, was identical with the slaver for whom their party was searching. Of this last he felt morally certain, for his deductions had, all through, proved much too correct to turn out utterly wrong in their final act: still it was a methodical and praiseworthy habit of his, born of his wide experience amongst criminals of every class, to impute nothing and to infer nothing which he could not prove up to the very hilt, and there were, moreover, personal facts arising from the explanation, facts of which his whole soul abhorred the revelation, and of which nothing short of the iron hand of stern necessity would persuade him to speak, even to Leigh.

By the camp fire that night the white men consulted long and earnestly, whilst their sable followers crouched near them in the gloom, in abject fear of the arrival of another unwelcome messenger from the mysterious rifles of their unseen foes.

Not one single instant would these black fellows have remained beside our two friends had they possessed even the ghost of a notion of where to run to, but to their terror-stricken minds the whole vast unknown of Central Africa, backed by their white masters, was preferable to facing the certainty of having to retrace their undefended steps through the Black Pass of the Dark Spirit of Evil, whose weird natural horrors were so ably seconded by unseen, but none the less unerring, marksmen.

The conclusion that Leigh and Kenyon ultimately came to was, that they had better coast round the slaver's supposed position in an easterly direction, making themselves thoroughly acquainted with the general run of the country, and keeping, meantime, their present distance from the pass, gradually work in a semicircle until they again reached the eastern exit of the kloof, when they would once more make a determined and final effort to fathom the secret of the place;

and in accordance with this resolution the little band struck their tents at daybreak, and to the delight of the natives once more turned their faces towards the rising sun.

For a full hour the little party marched cheerfully eastwards, and then their journeying in that direction was brought to a sudden and unpleasant end by the two leading natives disappearing into the ground without a moment's warning. No power on earth could save the wretched men, who vanished into the morass-- for such it was--ere any of the party had even time to stretch out a hand to help them.

The rest of the black fellows drew cautiously away, with their teeth chattering, and uttered cries indicative of intense fear, and no possible argument would induce any of them to again take the lead, so that Kenyon and Leigh had to get in front of the party and run the entire risk, whilst these cowards leisurely and safely followed them at a respectful distance.

The pair exercised very great caution, and soon grew to understand the signs of this immense swamp, which they now endeavoured to skirt in a northerly direction, and upon the dismal edge of which they camped again that night.

The days that followed were days of anxiety, not to say despair, for the very ground on which they trod would often shake and quiver beneath their tired feet, and the whole party scarce knew whether each step that was taken might not prove to be their last; and it was only after they had manfully struggled northwards for close upon a hundred miles that they were once more able to plant their feet on firm ground, and to breathe freely, with the knowledge that the treacherous swamp lay, at last, behind them.

After expending a couple of days in a much-needed rest, an experimental trip was made in a south-easterly direction, with the object of ascertaining if it were possible to force the slaver's supposed position by an advance in that quarter, but something less than three miles again brought the party into the dreaded swamp, from which they beat a hasty and undignified retreat.

For a whole weary day our friends marched due east, and then had the luck to fall in with a hunting party of friendly-disposed natives, from whom Kenyon learned that they must compass another two days' journey towards the rising sun, ere the swamp would permit them once more to travel southwards.

This quivering, quaking morass was known to the natives by an awful name, the nearest English equivalent for which appeared to be "the Mouth of Hell itself;" and a truly awful tract of country it was, and of a certainty merited most

24

thoroughly this infernal denomination.

These people knew nothing of any way through the marsh, and ridiculed the very notion of such a path existing, so that it was quite clear to our friends that many days of weary travel must elapse ere they could regain the eastern end of the kloof which they so eagerly sought to reach.

To add to the troubles of the little band, first Leigh and then the whole of their bearers, one after another, succumbed to swamp fever, and Kenyon, who entirely escaped its influence, had--as may well be imagined--his hands full for the next ten days. The American ascribed his own immunity from fever, to his having choked off the malarial microbes by almost incessant smoking, but if this view of the case were correct, Leigh should also have been let down very lightly, whereas the reverse obtained.

As soon as the men were sufficiently recovered to move, the whole party dragged their fevered forms a day's journey from the edge of the marsh, and again camping on high, firm ground, did simply nothing until they had in some measure regained both health and vigour, after which they more cheerfully resumed the road, and in another ten days were once again posted in their old location near the entrance to the pass, exercising the additional precaution, however, of walling in the camp with a particularly spiky and impenetrable zareba of thorn-bushes, and of placing a couple of men on guard at night.

The day following their arrival our friends decided to spend lazily in camp enjoying a thorough rest; and it was whilst Leigh was dozing and smoking by turns in the afternoon, that the ever active Kenyon stumbled, by the merest chance, upon an important discovery--no less, in fact, than the earnestly-desired key to the secret of the Black Pass. The matter fell out thus: Kenyon having nothing else to do, had, on the previous night developed several photographic negatives, and was now taking advantage of the sun to print off a number of pictures.

As each view came out of the printing frame, it was in turn examined and passed quickly into the fixing bath; but as he was, however, about to slip into the bath a view of the pass, he suddenly paused spell-bound, and forgetting his unfixed picture, held it in his hands, his eyes keenly noting every detail of the place. The strong light, of course, quickly turned the picture black, and with an exclamation of impatience he resumed his cool manner, printed and fixed another positive, then stowed away all his paraphernalia, and lighting his pipe, sat quietly down and gave his whole attention to the photograph.

After carefully studying the picture for close upon an hour, throwing now and again a keen glance at the gloomy-looking entrance to the kloof, he gave a grunt of satisfaction, and put the view into Leigh's ready hand, saying as he did so, "Well, old fellow, I have often heard the remark that photography cannot lie, but never until now have I realised the full force of the axiom. To-morrow, at daybreak, thanks to my camera, we shall enter Master Zero's mysterious territory, and then it will be diamond cut diamond with a vengeance."

Leigh was instantly alive with excitement, and this Kenyon quickly relieved by his explanation, which, aided as it was by the little picture, was as simple as it was lucid.

Chapter 5: The Secret of the Pass

The secret of the place, as revealed by the tell-tale photograph, existed simply in the perfect natural "blind" provided by the presence of the road through the pass, whilst the slaver's secret way was defined on the picture by a narrow wavy line, which absolutely wormed its way along the apparently unbroken face of the precipitous cliff itself, this way being primarily gained by climbing over the large, loose boulders which were freely strewed about just inside the entrance to the kloof. Gradually rising, and painfully zig-zagging up the giant wall of the rock, the narrow pathway could be clearly traced until it pierced the dark patch of brushwood which thickly crowned the summits of the towering cliffs, and was thenceforth lost to view. Deferring to Leigh's anxiety regarding his cousin, the pair left the camp as soon as the moon rose that night, and found, to their surprise, that they could easily climb the slaver's rocky road, and that what looked like a mere pathway for a goat, was in reality a well-worn track of a uniform width of from two and a half to three feet, and this being positively hollowed out to the depth of nearly a yard, made travelling perfectly safe, if not very fast. Human hands, at least in Central Africa, could never have accomplished such a stupendous task as this, and it was quickly evident to our friends that a small stream, running and zig-zagging down the cliff through the ages of bygone years, had gradually worn for itself a deep channel in the soft sandstone rock, and the lynx-eyed slaver had doubtless seen the value of the position, and on winning his way to the summit, in an abnormally dry season, had turned the stream into some other, and possibly more useful channel.

Proceeding with the utmost caution, and expecting every instant to receive the contents of a rifle through his ribs, Kenyon led the way up this strange ascent and in about forty minutes' time the pair had entered the dark and heavy patch of trees and brushwood which thickly crowned the cliffs, and which served, in some degree, to mask their true and enormous proportions. Arrived there, progress became of necessity slow, for it was only in places that the moonlight penetrated the interlaced tropic foliage, and threw ghostly patches of light and shade across the path of the adventurers, who drew nearer together as the painfully mysterious silence of the place impressed itself upon them.

It is not an altogether pleasant experience to find yourself alone at night in an ordinary English coppice or plantation, a mile or two from anywhere; but transplant that plantation into equatorial Africa, and stand there with the knowledge that you are hundreds of miles from even the nearest native village, people the wood with bloodthirsty foes, lurking, keen-eyed, in every brake and covert, armed with the treacherous spear or the ready rifle, and you will understand why Leigh and Kenyon, ordinarily bold enough in the open, could only creep forward with their hearts in their mouths, and felt an access of fear when a great owl, disturbed by their cautious passage through the wood, rose from the trees above them, waking the hush of night with a weird, spirit-shaking hoot, and winged his way far off into the moonlight, which was everywhere flooding the outside world with its mellow glory.

Soon, however, our friends again escaped from the lonely wooded path, and emerged into the brilliantly-lighted open, with a magnificent range of vision in every direction, except where the cliffs on the other side of the kloof shot upwards quite a hundred feet beyond the height of those now tenanted by themselves. This peculiarity, which the pair had not previously observed, of course effectually prevented them from seeing anything at all in the southern board, but in front and on each side of them the veldt could be seen sweeping clear away to the skyline, dotted here and there by clumps of bush and by moving herds of game. Behind them the mighty rocks frowned sternly down upon the adventurers, as if rebuking these weak creatures of an hour for disturbing with their puny presence the mist-beshrouded slumber of these mighty monarchs of all time.

After a short conference our friends withdrew again into the shadow of the wood, and sat themselves down to wait patiently for the dawn, talking all the time in a busy undertone, Leigh urging one plan of action, whilst Kenyon was seemingly quite determined upon taking a diametrically opposite course. Leigh wished, in fact, to move on at once towards the north, so as to remove their persons from the tell-tale heights before daybreak, whilst Kenyon was obstinately and aggressively desirous to know what lay behind the frowning wall of rock in their immediate rear, and as this meant re-descending the pass, and apparently crawling up the other side on their hands and knees, without any really definite object in view, Leigh's arguments certainly seemed the better.

"Why, Kenyon," he concluded, "do you want to change your mind? Formerly you were anxious to penetrate the swamp from an altogether impossible quarter in order to arrive at our present location, and now that you have a good open down-hill road before you, you are keen to turn your back upon it. At least, let me have your reason for this change of front."

"Simply this, Leigh," was the reply. "The pass itself, I now find, lies some-what to the north of the equator, and I am positively certain that the man we seek will be found in some place which lies absolutely on the equatorial line, con-sequently behind us, and therefore away on the other side of the kloof."

"But why, in the name of common-sense," persisted Leigh," should your man live on the equator, or near it at all? That's what I can't understand."

"See here, Leigh," was the cool answer; "that was my very first clue to this affair. He lives on latitude Number 0, otherwise Zero. Basing my whole theory and reasoning upon that, I have traced him to this spot, so I may fairly assume that my deductions are correct. However, sooner or later we shall have to investigate this side of the pass, so if you like we'll toss up when daylight comes, and let the coin decide for us."

Still unconvinced, though admiring the shrewdness of his comrade in following up a mere piece of guess-work, and elaborating it into such a strikingly correct theory, Leigh continued to urge his view of the matter, and soon the dawn came gliding over the earth, waking all nature with a kiss of peace, and preparing her for the advent of the glorious orb of day.

Chapter 6: Richard Grenville, His Mark

The daylight, however, told our friends nothing very new, only Kenyon hinted to Leigh that where the rocks below them levelled down to, and impinged upon, the veldt, everything was most suspiciously green and verdant, from which he inferred the presence of their old enemy, the marsh, in the immediate vicinity; then, turning round to examine the opposite cliff, his eye was caught by what seemed to be a curious kind of diagram engraved upon the face of the rock, perhaps two or three yards from the upper edge of one of its platforms, and scarce fifty feet away from them across the intervening chasm. The appearance it presented was as undernoted, the characters being some eighteen to twenty inches in length, and cut deeply into the soft sandstone with some apparently blunt instrument.

"Now," said Kenyon, calling his companion's attention to this, "what the deuce does yonder curious hieroglyphic signify? I've no knowledge of Arabic, but I think I'm right in saying that those signs belong to the calligraphy of no known language. To my professional eye they rather resemble a rough gibbet with three bodies hanging from it."

It so happened that, as soon as daylight had satisfied the pair that their foes were not hanging about in the immediate vicinity, Leigh had quietly laid himself down to enjoy a comfortable smoke, and was at the moment in question lying on the broad of his back, gazing at the wide vista of country below him, and puffing away in perfect tranquillity, with the apex of his skull pointing towards the chasm. To save himself the trouble of rising, he lazily elevated his chin, and performed the interesting occupation of looking, so to speak, over the top of his own head, and then electrified Kenyon by bounding to his feet with a wild hurrah, and shaking hands with him enthusiastically. "Found!" he fairly yelled. "Found, as sure as there is a heaven above us!"

"Why, confound it, old fellow," said Kenyon, ruefully nursing his bruised fingers, "whatever is the matter with you?"

"Matter!" was the reply. "Why, your hieroglyphic is as good as my cousin looking me in the face from yonder splendid rock. The solution of your mystery is a simple matter to me--a man, hanging head-downwards from yonder cliff, laboriously graved those curious characters, upside down, as we see them, upon the face of the rock, and the hand that wrote them was the hand of Grenville."

"And the meaning?" queried the attentive Kenyon, without showing any of his customary signs of incredulity or dissent.

"The hieroglyphic which is such a stumbling-block to you, Kenyon, simplified, stands thus:--

"I. v . LIII,

"and the meaning is merely `Richard Grenville.' It was a secret sign between my cousin and myself when we were mere schoolboys, and the simile was drawn from the memorable sea-fight in the reign of good Queen Bess, when Sir Richard Grenvil--God rest him for a gallant gentleman!--`with one small ship and his English few,' fought for a day and a night with fifty-three Spanish galleons. As a boy, my cousin-- though no descendant of the hero--was passionately devoted to this page of history, and used to sign himself `1 versus 53,' and so, by yonder sign, I know he lives, and lives looking for me to find him, and to read the hand he wrote, which to all others would, of course, be utterly unintelligible." And Leigh again set to and fairly danced with joy and excitement at this truly singular and fortunate discovery.

Whilst being thoroughly surprised, Kenyon could but congratulate himself at seeing the hall-mark of absolute accuracy thus unexpectedly stamped upon every link in the chain of his pet theory, and both men were now equally eager to descend the rocky pathway--the reason for the existence of this last being, under the circumstances, a positive enigma to them-- and recommence their search for the lost one on the other side of the kloof.

After a hasty breakfast, however, the pair decided that, as they were already on the spot, it would be best to thoroughly satisfy themselves regarding their own side of the chasm, more especially as, by the time they had descended the rocky pathway and called at the camp, it would have been too late to attempt the ascent of the cliffs, which were now believed by them to provide a rampart for the enemy, and a prison for their friend.

The twain, therefore, scrambled down the rocks facing towards the north, and quickly found, as Kenyon had predicted, that the position on that side was rendered altogether inaccessible by the presence of the swamp, which just here was very much in evidence. In every direction, as far as the eye could reach, it spread itself out brightly verdant and inviting in the sunshine, but utterly treacherous and unstable, and the nearer it approached to the rocks the more palpable did the fraud appear, as, at the point where the stony ground impinged upon the veldt, the swamp was little better than stagnant pools of slimy, evil-smelling water, overgrown with reeds and rushes.

Re-ascending the rocks, Leigh and Kenyon sheltered themselves in the woods from the rays of the vertical sun, utilising their time by making themselves, as they believed, thoroughly conversant with the place, and when the day began to grow towards evening, they left the bush-clothed heights, and again turned their faces towards the camp.

Just as the pair commenced the descent of the narrow rocky path Kenyon suddenly paused, and drew in his breath with an angry hiss, and following the direction of his eager gaze, Leigh looked towards their tent, which was plainly in view, about a mile away as the crow flies.

From the height at which our friends stood, they had, of course, an unrestricted view of the plain stretched out before them, and everything upon it, and there, some two hundred yards from the camp, and clearly outlined against the veldt upon which he lay stretched, was the unwelcome figure of an unmistakable spy, who, so far as he could be made out at that distance, wore the garments of a white man.

When he had spent quite half-an-hour in this position, and no doubt thoroughly taken stock of his surroundings, the fellow was seen to turn and worm his way back, until he obtained the cover of a low clump of bush about a quarter of a mile from the camp, and was thenceforward hidden from sight.

After some little time had elapsed, and as our friends were debating what steps they had best take, a fresh surprise was provided for them, as the pair distinctly saw a snow-white pigeon leave the bush in question, describe one or two airy circles round it, and then wing its way directly towards the cliffs across the kloof, beyond which it quickly disappeared.

"A carrier pigeon, by Jove!" said Kenyon, "doubtless bearing a request to Master Zero to come down and cut all our throats to-night. All right, my friend, forewarned is forearmed, and you'll find it so this evening, unless I am very much mistaken."

Carefully getting down to the exit of the pass, the twain commenced a cautious stalk, and came in upon their quarry just at dusk, and great was the astonishment and consternation of the wretched spy when the two men quietly rose from the long grass, and, covering him with their revolvers, peremptorily ordered him to lay down his arms; this he promptly did in most abject fashion, and was in two minutes bound hard and fast with his own lasso, of which most objectionable instrument his armament consisted, backed up by a long American muzzle-loading rifle and a light axe or tomahawk.

The captive was apparently a Spaniard, as he protested volubly in that language--of which Kenyon had a smattering--against the gratuitous outrage committed upon his unoffending person.

Suddenly, taking advantage of an instant when neither of his captors had their eyes on him, the fellow darted to one side, and gave a kick at some small object which our friends had passed unnoticed in the long grass; this object, however, proved to be a little wicker basket, and from this receptacle--its prison doors thrown open by the intentional violence of its owner--there fluttered a large, black pigeon, which circled round the heads of the party and prepared to take its flight, just as its white predecessor had previously done. Fortunately, the bird was dazed and confused by the blow it had received, and hovered round the spot an instant too long. Like a flash Leigh's rifle went to his shoulder, and the next second the bird lay in a lifeless heap upon the ground, whilst the spy ground out a bitter Spanish curse.

The shot was a very fine one, and but few men could have accomplished it with a repeating-rifle and a single bullet, but its success had, without a doubt, prevented the spy from giving to his friends or followers inopportune notice of his capture and detention.

Quickly proceeding into camp, where the rifle-shot had set their men buzzing about like bees, a hasty meal was partaken of, and then, leaving the tent still standing, the whole party, upwards of twenty-five in number, at once set out for the pass, as our friends believed that if they could once get their men up to the top of the rocky path, they would easily be able to hold the wood and the steep and narrow way against all comers. Finding it a matter of impossibility to get any information out of the captive, they gagged him and walked him off with them, Kenyon sternly telling him that if he tried to make any noise or attempted to escape, he would run a hunting-knife through his ribs without further notice.

By the time the moon rose the party had stumbled out their way to the mouth of the kloof, and soon had sufficient light to commence the ascent. Having to go in front and lead the way, Kenyon put Leigh in the rear to see that none of the bearers lost heart and turned back, giving the captive into the charge of a gigantic Zanzibari, and warning him that did he let the man go he should himself be shot like a dog. All went well until the party was quite two-thirds of the way up the zig-zag in the rock, when suddenly a commotion arose, and a cry went up that the prisoner was escaping. Turning angrily round, with his revolver half raised, Kenyon saw the spy standing on the very edge of the parapet of rock, with his hands at liberty, and in the act of drawing the gag from his mouth. On seeing Kenyon turn, the Zanzibari doubtless thought he was himself about to be shot, and impelled by rage and fear, he sprang wildly upon the ledge of rock and seized the Spaniard by the throat. Forgetting the extreme danger of his position, the white man swayed backwards to strike an effective blow at his sable assailant, overbalanced, and down they both went, with a horrid scream that rang out far into the stilly night, and awakened long-drawn, fearsome echoes in the dark and silent kloof.

One second more, and the horror-stricken band of listeners heard the united bodies of the ill-fated pair strike with a sickening scrunch on the rocks five hundred feet below. The whole affair was over in an instant of time, and even the stem detective was deeply impressed by this awful dual fatality, and could only beckon with his hand for the others to follow him upwards quickly and in silence.

In a few moments more the adventurers emerged from the rocky path and gained the shelter of the bushes, where Leigh and Kenyon quickly bestowed the men in safe covers, and then posted themselves at a point from which they could command the other side of the kloof, and so possibly form an opinion as to how their enemies scaled its heights; for at a glance the ascent gave promise of providing them with an extremely difficult, if not impossible, task, and if, in addition to negotiating this, they had to cope en route with an armed and intrenched foe, the prospect of success would be extremely problematical.

Leigh had a theory that the slavers were provided with long rope-ladders, but arguing from the rapid disappearance of the slave caravan, Kenyon declared that this suggestion would not hold water for a moment.

Scarcely had Leigh and Kenyon gained their covers than, to their utter astonishment, steps were heard approaching through the wood in their rear, and whilst they were making themselves as small as possible, and breathing a devout prayer that the black fellows might not lose their heads and try to run away, a band of armed men passed swiftly by their position and emerged into the moonlight.

The new-comers were about thirty in number, all armed with axe, rifle, and lasso, and were, with but two or three exceptions, white men. As they reached the zig-zag pass, the party extended into single file and promptly disappeared from view down the face of the rock. Until all had vanished Kenyon scarcely breathed, then Leigh and he turned eagerly to one another, and hurriedly and anxiously discussed the situation.

Their examination that very day of the side of the kloof upon which they now stood had been much too complete to admit of their believing that the men who had just passed them had been all the time lying hid, and the inference naturally was that these strange people had some peculiar method of crossing the gorge at its upper edge. Such an apparently preposterous idea had, of course, not occurred to the pair when searching the wood, but had the path been at all easy to find they would most certainly have stumbled across it.

Moving quietly along the back track, the pair cautiously examined every likely spot, and were about to enter a particularly black-looking clump of bush, when they were suddenly brought to a standstill by the gruff challenge of a colossal-looking sentry, who started out from the dark background of wood and threateningly raised his rifle.

"Halt! Halt! And give the password!"

Leigh's hand stole towards his revolver; but men think rapidly in emergencies like this, and in a moment of inspiration, Kenyon coolly answered, "Zero!"

"Pass, Zero, and all's well," grunted the gigantic sentinel, grounding his arms with a clash, and then, in a theatrical whisper as the pair approached him, "Mates, you haven't got a drink on you, have you? It's main cold up here."

Quickly Leigh held out his flask, and as the other was in the very act of drinking, Kenyon flew at his throat like a cat, and choked him down, whilst Leigh knelt on his chest, and tried to bind him. Our friends were both exceptionally powerful men, but this fellow was a regular bull of Bashan, and it was only after a low whistle had summoned one of their native guides that the trio got the sentry bound and gagged to their satisfaction. Next, sending the black fellow to keep watch at the top of the zig-zag, the pair set to to thoroughly explore the tangled path which had been guarded by the sentry. A most unpleasant task this was, too, feeling their way about on the very verge of an immense precipice, thickly clothed with trees and bush, through which the rays of the moon cast at intervals a sickly glamour of feeble light and heavy shade.

At last a brief exclamation from Leigh announced a discovery, and standing by his side, and looking directly across the chasm, Kenyon saw a curious, and in its way, a striking spectacle. From one side of the kloof to the other stretched the taut strands of a mighty double rope or hawser, and from this rope was suspended

35

a small cage, capable of containing two or three men, the occupants drawing themselves across by small guide-ropes, whilst the cage moved easily along the hawser upon wheeled blocks, the whole arrangement being entirely concealed from the view of anyone, either above or below, by the trees on either side of the chasm, which at this point blended and interlaced both their foliage and their branches.

So far good, but as the cage now swung in mid-air over the very centre of the chasm itself, and had, moreover, an occupant, it was difficult to see what the next move was to be. It was, however, our friends reflected, at all events consoling to know that a slash or two with a sharp knife would effectually dispose of all possibility of their savage foes attacking them in the rear.

Just at this moment a cautious whistle told Kenyon that danger was to be apprehended from the direction of the veldt, but at that very instant the man in the cage, evidently thinking that the signal had been given for his benefit, commenced to haul upon the rope, and quickly gaining their side of the chasm, leaped out right into the ready arms of the pair, who very soon had him securely gagged and tied to a tree, at a little distance from his fellow. Hurrying back as another low but earnest whistle reached their ears, our friends found that the slavers had been seen to surround the tent, and thoroughly explore it; then, evidently disliking the look of things, they had set out at speed towards the pass, which they must now be in the very act of climbing.

Carrying off the whole frightened crowd, with the exception of one man who had shown himself a tolerable marksman and something removed from an abject coward, Kenyon showed them how to cross the chasm safely and quietly, and bade them get over at once with all the ammunition. Persuasion and explanation was, however, of no use at all, and he had to drive the first batch into the strange vehicle at the muzzle of his revolver. Then, finding they were quite safe, the negroes promptly commenced to chatter like so many monkeys, whereupon Kenyon threatened to shoot them, if he heard another sound, and then returned with all expedition to Leigh, who had posted himself so as to command the zig-zag, and had cleverly rolled a big rock into the very mouth of the channel by which the foe was approaching.

All was now in readiness, and a dead silence reigned. The hush of a tranquil tropical midnight was upon everything, and all nature was looking her loveliest under the glamour of the shimmering moonlight. All at once the stillness was marred by a footfall, and then rent, as it were, by a furious curse, as the leading slaver reached the top of the pass, and found the way blocked up. Climbing carefully over the stone, however, he safely reached terra firma, and was stooping down to remove the obstruction, when he was angrily hailed in nervous English by Kenyon--"Here, you dog, leave that stone alone, and go back by the way you came. Quickly now, and drop that rifle--drop it, I say, or your blood be on your own head!"

For answer, the fellow fired point-blank in the direction of the voice (for he could not see Kenyon, who was standing in the shadows of the wood), and then made for cover, but he never reached it; indeed, he had hardly moved in his tracks, when down he went, as dead as a door-nail, being followed a moment later, along the same dark and fearsome road, by a comrade who persisted in obtruding over the rock rather more of his person than Leigh was disposed to permit, and ere the thundering echoes of the rifles had ceased to answer and to mock one another amongst the surrounding rocks, the remainder of the slavers, having no more stomach for such work, were in full retreat down the rock, and half an hour later were seen steering wide out into the south-western veldt, thus putting entirely to rest any doubts which Kenyon still entertained of the feasibility of an attempt to scale the opposite cliffs.

Had there been any way of ascending on the other side of the kloof, it was quite certain the slavers would have known about it, whereas they had clearly found it necessary to make a very wide circuit in order to get round the rocks, and thus make their way back to head-quarters.

Sending forward their sable supporters with instructions to get the prisoners across the chasm, Kenyon led his wondering comrade up the cliffs to the right, where they suddenly came upon a small lake, obviously fed by a neighbouring mountain stream.

"Now, old fellow," said he, "just lay down your rifle, and help me to break up this wall, and assist outraged nature to regain her ancient rights."

Leigh quickly saw that the water, which came sweeping rhythmically down from the further heights beyond the hill, had at this point been artfully turned by a well-made wall, built of rock and broken stone, and apparently strengthened with mortar or cement, so that the stream, instead of exercising its own sweet will by zig-zagging down the rock, as it had done of yore, was wasted on the north-western veldt, where its advent had probably been largely responsible for the origination of the marsh, which had already given our friends such a world of trouble. The wall of the dam, however, proved considerably stronger than

Kenyon had bargained for, so they finally bored a hole in it, and blew the whole affair up with a couple of flasks of powder taken from the fallen slavers.

When the smoke of the explosion cleared away, the released water could be seen bounding over the rocks, and shooting down the narrow channel with a wild, sweeping rush, effectually closing this method of ascending the cliffs unless in abnormally dry seasons. A moment later and our friends could see the stream filtering along its old course across the veldt, looking like a mighty silver snake as it gleamed and twisted on its tortuous way, reflecting at every turn the brilliancy of the lovely crescent moon.

Regaining the edge of the kloof, our friends stepped into the cage, and were soon hauled across the chasm by one of their men, who was already quite expert in this singular method of semi-aerial procedure.

On examining the prisoners Kenyon was disgusted to find that they were both stone dead, the cowardly blacks having killed them, bound as they were, lest the slavers should get loose and do them an injury. This was the more aggravating, as Kenyon had fairly counted upon forcing information of some kind out of the men, and he was, besides, disposed to think well of the big sentry who had hailed them in English. However, the men were dead, and it was, therefore, useless regretting them, but Kenyon inwardly registered a vow to get even with the rascal who had committed such a brace of infernally cold-blooded murders should he ever find him out. Then sternly ordering the men to shoulder their loads, the party set out under the waning moon, directing their steps downwards and towards the south-east.

Chapter 7: Just in Time

For quite a quarter of a mile our friends found that the road provided very rough travelling indeed. This was the more annoying, as the moon was fast going down, and it was a matter of vital importance that the little band should progress quickly and secure a strong position before daylight revealed their movements to the enemy.

Their only difficulty would be with regard to water, as the party had an abundant supply of stores and ammunition; for, having, of course, no idea as to how long the expedition might be detained in the Interior, Leigh had provisioned it most lavishly, and as game had hitherto been plentiful, the stores had been very lightly dealt with.

In an hour's time all had, as they thought, reached level ground, for the road, after the first half-mile had been negotiated, proved fairly good, and finding a lofty cavern in the rock, Kenyon drew his whole party into it, cast anchor, and wished for the day.

The darkness had now become positively opaque, for the moon had entirely disappeared behind the mountains, and a film of mist seemed everywhere to hang over the lower lands, and had their enemies been absolutely within arm's length, our friends would have been utterly unable to distinguish them.

Soon, however, the "darkest hour" was over, and the eastern mountains became dimly outlined through the gauze-like curtain of mist, as the glad light of another brilliant day came speeding in upon the wings of the morning, heralding the advent of the sun himself with all the attendant splendour of an equatorial African day.

Our friends at once perceived that, so far from having reached the level of the country, they were at present posted on a ridgy platform upon the mountain side, whilst far below them, the land which lay considerably lower than that on the other side of the kloof, was stretched out before them in wonderfully beautiful panorama.

On one hand a limpid stream glided peacefully along its course, making dreamland music in the sunshine, and watering mile after mile of verdant pasture land, which was dotted hero and there with moving herds of game, whilst on the other was a mighty belt of giant forest trees, backed to the eastward by the everlasting mountains, which appeared absolutely to ring-in the country in that direction, though towards the west, as far as the eye could reach, only grass land could be seen, the rolling veldt sweeping clear away to the skyline unrelieved by even a single clump of trees or bush, and broken only here and there by the silvery tracery of tiny streamlets; whilst to the south, blue in the far distance and faintly relieved against the azure setting of the sky, could be traced the dim outline of a giant mountain-peak, probably fifteen thousand feet in height, its snow-capped crest flashing back in many-coloured radiance each glorious spear of light cast by the rising sun.

Kenyon and Leigh were about to give the word to their men (all of whom were busily gazing at the inviting prospect before them) to get under weigh, when both were fairly electrified by hearing a voice raised in the cavern just behind them.

"Greeting!" it said; "greeting to ye strangers." Then as our friends turned quickly round, and their white personality became evident to the speaker, "Greeting, white strangers, who come from the northern lands beyond the distant seas. What seek ye here in this foul place, where all things that are good live but to die, and where only evil prospers, and the arch-fiend himself bears rule? What seek ye here with Muzi Zimba the old? and ye black ones, are ye tired of life, and of that freedom which alone makes life worth living, that ye venture your heads inside the lion's mouth? Go I go, all of ye, white and black. Go! in God's name, while the life is yet whole in ye. Why tarry ye here? Escape for your lives, my sons, and peace go with ye."

Our friends had been closely watching the individual who delivered this strange yet forcible appeal, and looks of commiseration passed from one to the other. The man was as white-skinned as themselves, and judging from the purity of his English must have been at one time a British subject. He was, however, extremely old, probably eighty-five or ninety, and his face, which was benign and gentle, was shrouded by his long, silvery locks, and muffled, as it were, in an immense snow-white beard, which reached down to his very waist, and gave him an altogether venerable and striking appearance; his voice was strong and resonant, his manner quiet and peaceful, but the man was obviously mad. He had evidently become so accustomed to the native metaphor that he had unconsciously adopted it as his own language, and his diction at best halted somewhat, as if he were unused, indeed, to exercising his tongue in framing speech of any kind.

Whilst Kenyon hesitated what to do, Leigh went frankly forward and held but his hand to the old fellow, who shook it heartily; then, humouring him, Leigh spoke, and as the full, rich voice struck upon his ear, the old man bent his head and seemed as if the familiar accents had brought back to him some signs or memories of the long-forgotten past.

"Greeting, my father, greeting," answered Leigh. "Thy sons have wandered hither on a long and very weary path, seeking for a lost one who left them many moons ago. In face he was even as I am, and in form was somewhat less, and spoke to his people with an English tongue. Tell me, hast thou seen such an one, my father?"

The old man gazed steadily at Leigh for some moments, then, changing his wrapt manner, he spoke sadly, "My son, I have, indeed, met with him, and thy living image he was; but never, alas! Wilt thou see him in the flesh, for to-day he dies--ay! Dies a dog's death, and does it for his faith, like a gallant Christian man."

"Dies?" thundered Leigh; "he shall not die, he must not die--oh! Dick, Dick, have I come right across the world to arrive one day too late?"

Eagerly the pair tried to question the old man, but he at once grew confused and his weak mind evidently failed to realise their anxiety or to grasp the drift of their questions, and at last he turned upon them with quiet dignity. "Leave me now, my sons," he said, "for I go to offer prayers for him who dies when yonder sun reaches the zenith. Return whence ye came, so shall ye live and not die--go, and God go with ye--farewell!" and this strange individual moved slowly away down the cavern and disappeared in the inner gloom.

Hastily directing their men to lie hidden in the cave until their return, Leigh and Kenyon armed themselves to the teeth, and quickly slipping down the rocky path, were soon speeding across the open, and directing their hurried steps towards the forest.

Each was equipped with a repeating-rifle, four Smith and Wesson's revolver-pistols, and as much ammunition as he could well carry, so that the pace, in spite of the best endeavours of the pair, was somewhat slow, and when, after two hours of continued effort, they entered the belt of wood, both judged it expedient to sit down and eat some food whilst enjoying a short rest. Soon, however, getting on their legs again, our friends struck into a forest path, which they followed as fast as they could travel, instinct, or else the promptings of despair

41

leading them in the right direction.

For another hour the pair ascended gradually through the forest, the path leading steadily upwards, and ultimately terminating in a sharp climb; but, just as they were about to negotiate this piece of wooded rock, they heard a burst of music [sic] evidently proceeding from tom-toms, horns, and other instruments of abomination, dear to the heart of the aboriginal African.

Cautiously ascending the rock, our friends concealed themselves in a bush, and then a curious sight met their eyes. Some thirty feet below them lay a sort of hollow in the mountains, which looked as if it had at one time formed the base of a vast quarry, being perhaps a thousand yards across its widest part, and shaped somewhat in the form of a horseshoe, but now carpeted everywhere with short, smooth turf. At the farther side of this mighty enclosure was a narrow gap or pass in the mountains, which clearly gave access to the spot, and through this striking natural gateway some thousands of ebony-skinned Africans were now pouring, accompanying their march with all sorts of horrible and ear-splitting native music.

Quickly the black fellows filed in, to the number of, probably, three thousand, and squatted themselves down on the rocks, which, as on the side occupied by Leigh and his comrade, formed a solid barrier some thirty feet high round the ring of level turf.

Following upon the heels of this riff-raff appeared a mixed mob of some three to four hundred white men and women, escorting a native who was evidently a King, or, at least, a "Big Chief," judging from the attentions they lavished upon him, and from his striking "get up." This last consisted of a stove-pipe hat, a scarlet coat adorned with gold braid, and a pair of bright yellow stockings of unusual length, reaching well up the thigh; round his waist was buckled an enormously long cavalry sword, which trailed upon the ground as he walked, and in his hand he carried a "gun" considerably taller than himself; it was, in fact, one of those fearfully and wonderfully made specimens of the genus gas-pipe with which England and Germany delight to arm the whole of Africa at about eight shillings per head.

"Solomon in all his glory, by Jove," whispered Leigh to the observant and attentive Kenyon. All disposition to laugh was, however, quickly stifled by the appearance of a man carrying a flag, which was promptly planted in the very centre of the open space, and welcomed by the assembled thousands with a positive frenzy of enthusiasm, but was greeted by Leigh with a groan of horror and dismay, for upon a dead black ground it bore a white circle, and in the centre of this ring were three horrible basilisk-looking eyes.

Kenyon on his part whistled quietly. "So!" he said, "Zero and the Mormon Trinity--birds of a feather, by all that's holy! Well, we must watch and wait, and somehow I don't think our patience will be tried for very much longer."

Just then a hammock was borne in, and from this there alighted a white woman, a Spaniard or an Italian by her looks; this female being instantly accommodated with a seat, and approached with much deference by the white men in the crowd.

Leigh thought he had never seen a more wicked, yet withal a more handsome, face. Her complexion was beautifully clear, her hair black and glossy as the raven's wing, and her figure simply superb; but the eyes looked like coals of living fire, and the mouth, as Kenyon--who was busy sketching her in his notebook--remarked, was more like a spring rat-trap than anything else.

A wait of half an hour next ensued, during which the native band discoursed sweet (?) music, and then there went up a mighty shout from the motley throng which thickly lined the farther side of the great enclosure, as a small crowd of men, white and black, were driven in at the spear's point; all had their hands tied behind them, but had their legs left perfectly free to enable them to run at will, the slavers knowing well, that deprived as the captives were of the use of their hands and arms, they could not escape by climbing up the rocks.

A moment later the friends, to their utter horror, beheld a barrier lifted, and through the opening thus made there immediately charged a colossal-looking bull-elephant. For a full minute the great brute gazed wickedly about him, as if debating the possibility of getting at the block fellows who were rapidly angering him with their infernal tom-toms; next he trumpeted until the welkin rang again, and then all of a sudden threw up his trunk, and hurled his vast bulk blindly at the wretched band of captives, who fled incontinently in every direction, whilst the air resounded with yells of laughter from the spectators, black and white, across the wide enclosure. These wretches were evidently enjoying to the full this intensely Roman spectacle, and Leigh felt his blood boil at the thought that the lives of human beings--white men, moreover--were to be deliberately sacrificed in this truly diabolical manner to provide an hour's amusement for an ignorant savage and his greasy, yelping retinue of semi-monkeyfied followers. By and by, however, a great black man fleeted--with the speed of light--past the rock where our friends lay hid, the enraged elephant following close upon his heels; and brief

43

though the glimpse was, in an instant Leigh knew his man, and blew a peculiar little reed whistle which Kenyon had often noticed attached to his friend's watch-chain.

Once! Twice! Thrice! He sounded the signal, and then, lo! and behold, every captive on the ground, both white and black, was seen to turn short in his tracks and speed madly across the wide stretch of open, in a wild endeavour to reach the distant rock; close behind the crowd thundered the giant mammal, screaming with rage, and gaining upon the luckless wights at every step, the tip of his snake-like trunk almost seeming to touch the hindmost runner. It was an altogether extraordinary, yet at the same time a very dreadful, sight; and as Leigh's rifle leaped to his shoulder, he seemed, by one of those curious tricks which fancy sometimes plays us, to see the Colosseum spread out before him, its benches packed to suffocation with the pleasure-seekers of an ancient Roman holiday, and its arena peopled by the noble martyrs falling beneath the claws of Nero's ravening beasts.

History ever repeats itself, and at this very instant, whilst the easy-going people of the nineteenth Christian century were sitting quietly in their peaceful homes, thanking God that such acts and deeds were forever at an end, here was the horrid self-same spectacle being re-enacted in darkest Africa, without any of the added refinements of modern cruelty, upon the living bodies of their own fellow-men, both white and black.

Thought, however, is swift, and Leigh's thought delayed him never an instant, and even as he pressed the trigger and saw the deadly bullet go home, and the mighty elephant pitch forward upon his knees, he sprang upright upon the ledge of rock, to show the captives where their friends lay hid; then, as his rifle thundered out again, backed up by the echo of Kenyon's heavy piece, and the discomfited elephant wallowed on the ground with three shell bullets in his ugly carcass, Leigh was conscious that Kenyon was slipping down the rock, and quickly following his friend, both were in an instant busy with their hunting-knives upon the thongs which held the prisoners, who, twenty-five in number, six white and the rest black, were all at liberty and eagerly scrambling up the rock before the mixed assemblage beyond the great enclosure had thoroughly realised what was going on, less than a thousand yards away, under cover of the smoke and the rapid discharges of strange rifles.

Just as a crowd of white men came streaming across the ground, and as Leigh was about to raise his rifle with the view of checking their advance, a voice behind him said, "Give me a turn at that, Alf; I long to get even with yonder blasphemous slaving hound. He tarred and feathered me one day."

Leigh knew the voice, and turning quickly, confronted his long-lost Cousin Dick. One warm hand-grasp was all, then the tears started to his eyes, as he relinquished his gun and strode away.

Dick Grenville! But alas! How changed--feeble, emaciated, and hollow-eyed, covered with filth, and clad in the skin of a leopard. Leigh had actually taken his own cousin for a very ordinary-looking black man, but the old spirit, unbroken by Mormons or slavers, was still there--the eye as true, and the hand firm as a grip of steel. Springing forward, he shook the weapon over his head, and his voice went ringing across the rock-bound stretch of veldt, as he called to the leader of the advancing crowd, "Crewdson Walworth, I promised you this a year ago, and here it is--a Grenville ever keeps his word." The rifle vomited its deadly contents, and the man, who was none other than Kenyon's quondam acquaintance, the "Swell" of Durban, went down, with a bullet through his heart, and pitched head over heels like a shot rabbit.

Kenyon coolly followed up the shot, and the repeaters fairly opened a lane in the approaching crowd, who fired wildly into the bush without doing any serious damage, and in another moment, to the number of about twenty, were busy scrambling up the rock, whilst Leigh, Grenville and Kenyon emptied rifle and revolver into their ranks at point-blank range. Suddenly Leigh heard another well-remembered voice. "Let my father," it said, "give Amaxosa a little space, that the child of the Undi may revenge himself, and slay these evil-minded men;" and moving to one side, Leigh saw his oft-tried comrade-in-arms, the proud young Zulu chief, walk coolly to the very verge of the platform, with a mighty mass of rock poised in his powerful arms. For one brief instant he stood thus, while his keen eye played over the hated forms of his late masters; then with a wild, earth-shaking shout he plunged the enormous missile right into the midst of the enemy where they were most closely massed together, bearing them backwards to the ground a bleeding, senseless pulp of human flesh and bones.

The revolvers quickly accounted for the few men who were left alive, and a minute later the re-united cousins, led by Kenyon, and followed by their triumphant "Impi," were descending the rock on its outer side, and making for the friendly cover of the forest, their only loss being one Zulu, who was shot through the body, and whom necessity compelled them to leave behind at the point of dissolution.

A hasty consultation ensued when the whole party had reached the forest, and both Leigh and Kenyon heard, with unmixed satisfaction, that the enemy would be under the necessity of following directly upon their trail, there being absolutely no path by which he could get round or cut off the retreat of the fugitives. Grenville also added that his friends had come in a fortunate hour, for had Zero himself been present, or had Crewdson Walworth not fallen so early in the fray, all would have had their work cut out to get away from the enclosure with whole skins. So weak were the late captives, that travelling was of necessity very slow indeed, or at least it seemed so to men fleeing with the knowledge that re-capture meant prompt and certain death.

Owing to the villainous treatment he had received, poor Grenville was in a pitiable state, but after a twenty minutes' rest, during which his cousin fed him with biscuits steeped in brandy, he made another effort, and Kenyon having speeded on ahead, and chased down their bearers with a hammock, the party soon had Grenville safely and comfortably housed in their temporary lodging on the mountain side.

Here the rescued one assured them that the whole band might safely lie hidden for a day or two during Zero's absence, as both white and black slavers held the spot in superstitious veneration on account of the presence of the old hermit--for some such thing Grenville declared their mad friend of the morning to be. Half priest he was, half doctor, and partly recluse. Grenville knew naught of him beyond the fact that he had occupied his present location, and been looked up to by the natives as a species of god, long years before ever Zero and his following of scoundrels overran the country side. For his simple necessities he received weekly supplies at the hands of the surrounding negro chiefs, who held him to be the greatest fetish in the land, and believed that he could kill or cure them, ruin their crops, or give them rain and fruitful seasons at his will; not that he, poor old man, had ever attempted to inoculate them with any such belief, having, on the contrary, always treated them as kindly as if they were his own children. To Grenville he had been extremely good, and had seemed much impressed with him, because our friend hod once again refused to buy his life at the prohibitive price of an introduction into the Mormon brotherhood.

Kenyon had tried to give Grenville in few words the history of his cousin's bereavement, fearing that a natural, yet abrupt, inquiry after Lady Drelincourt would greatly distress poor Leigh. The detective found, however, to his astonishment, that Grenville was in possession of full particulars of the cowardly double murder, Zero having boasted to him of the commission of the deed as a meritorious action, performed in revenge for the doings of their own party in East Utah. The slaver-chieftain had, it appeared, possessed himself of the persons of Grenville and of Amaxosa and some thirty of his warriors, by a skilfully-executed night attack, in which he was supported by upwards of three hundred armed whites and a horde of natives.

The story of the captives after this date was written in letters of torture and of blood, and when his cousin, to try him, asked Grenville how soon he would be in condition to turn his face homewards, the old spirit blazed out once more, as he vowed by all he held sacred that he would never leave the locality until Zero and his villainous following were completely wiped out and stamped flat, even did he know that his own life would in consequence be forfeited.

Needless to say, both Leigh and Kenyon heard these determined expressions with undisguised satisfaction, for these two had already come secretly to a like unanimous decision, and being now assisted by Grenville, with his perfect local knowledge, and backed by several white men, in addition to the redoubtable Amaxosa and a score of his picked warriors, who only required a few days of rest and good food to fit them for anything at all in the fighting line, both men felt much more sanguine of accomplishing the end they had in view, and of meting out stern retributive justice to the villainous slavers, and the double-dyed murderer who acted as their chief.

Asked to relate how he had executed the hieroglyphic upon the face of the rock within the kloof, Grenville explained that he had been bound at the "tail-end" of a line of half-a-dozen Zulus, and thrown upon the ground at the very edge of the cliff, whilst the slavers were bringing up the rest of their wretched captives by moonlight, and getting a sharp stone in his fettered hands, he had hung, head-downwards, suspended over the gulf in perfect safety, knowing that the weight of the men above would be a sheet-anchor for him. To Grenville's dismay, however, he found, when his work was done, that he could not regain his position on the rock, and just as he was losing consciousness with the rush of blood to his head, he was rescued by the slavers, who flogged him soundly for what they took to be a deliberate attempt to rob them of his valued person by the committal of cold-blooded suicide.

Cautious as ever, Grenville could not be persuaded to rest or sleep until he had seen Leigh and Amaxosa on guard, and had warned Kenyon to relieve the Zulu chief in two or three hours, as the poor fellow had had, he said, an uncommonly rough time of it lately, and the diabolical and senseless ill-usage to which he had been subjected, must have told its tale upon even his iron constitution.

The rest of the white men and Zulus, all of whom Leigh had been able to arm out of his ample stores of weapons, were already sleeping such a sleep as they had not enjoyed for a full year. To Grenville's delight, he found that his cousin had got a spare Winchester rifle for him, and with this and a pair of his favourite revolvers, he felt fit and ready for anything once again.

Chapter 8: Zero

Though quietly settled down for the night, our friends had yet, however, to learn that they hod not altogether done with the Mormon-cum-Slaver fraternity, who evidently could not rest satisfied, or allow the day to close, without making a particularly abominable attempt to get even with the fugitives and their new-found friends.

In the very dead of night, as Leigh and Amaxosa stood on guard at the mouth of the cave, conversing in an undertone, they were treated to a new and extremely objectionable sample of the qualities of their detested foes. The fire behind them inside the cavern had completely burnt itself out, and close to its ashes lay Grenville, sleeping heavily, whilst the other members of the party were scattered about the cave on beds of moss or dried grass. Not a sound of any kind betokening the presence of a foe had the anxious watchers heard, when all of a sudden both were startled into action by an angry hiss just behind them, followed by the well-known and universally dreaded "skirr" of a rattlesnake, and quickly lighting a torch of twisted grass, the pair saw the horrid reptile gliding down the cave towards them, evidently making for the entrance. Seizing a native sword, Amaxosa rushed at the snake with a wild shout. Instantly the reptile stopped in its tortuous course, and reared itself to strike, but the active Zulu was altogether too quick for it, and, with one fell sweep of his keen weapon, drove its head clean from its body, when something was heard to roll with a hollow, bell-like sound upon the rocky floor.

As Amaxosa's voice went ringing up the arches of the cavern, each occupant had sprung to his feet in an instant, with arms in his hands, and Grenville was himself the first to step forward and pick up the article, the fall of which had caused the ringing noise referred to. He gave but a single glance at this hollow, silver ring, for such it was, and then handed it to the Zulu chief, with the one word, "Apollyon!"

"Ay! Inkoos," was the answer, "I saw the shining circlet ere I struck, and the sight lent strength to my arm, for well I knew that if the blow did not go home I should not live to strike again. Glad am I, my father, that yon evil beast is dead, for I ever feared it more than I feared the evil ones themselves."

Grenville then explained to Kenyon and the wonder-stricken Leigh that this horrible reptile was a pet snake, kept by the white woman they had that day seen in the enclosure, and who, going by the name of Zero's wife, was at this time the dominating female spirit of the Mormon Community in Equatoria, as the adjacent slave-town was called. This infernal nineteenth-century harpy had made the snake, "Apollyon," her peculiar care, and by continual practice upon ailing or dying slaves had trained it to follow a trail, and to fix itself upon any person of whom she gave it the scent, quite as surely, and infinitely more quietly and fatally, than even Zero's own particular bloodhounds. It was self-evident that the reptile had been commissioned to destroy Grenville, and would most certainly have succeeded in doing so had not an all-merciful Providence willed otherwise. Unfortunately for the snake, it had drawn its loathsome coils right across the spot where the fire had recently been blazing, and, although the wood had quite burnt itself out, the floor of the cave was still absolutely red-hot, and the whole stomach of the snake was in consequence terribly scorched and blistered, and the sudden agony had no doubt caused it to emit the warning hiss which had put Amaxosa on his guard, whilst the severe nature of its injuries had probably contributed, in no small degree, to the success of his attack, by rendering the motions of the reptile unusually slow and extremely painful. Anyhow, it was a miraculous and providential escape, for which all felt uncommonly thankful, and Leigh heard with unconcealed satisfaction that the snake in question was positively the only one so trained which the vindictive Madame Zero had in her possession.

This unpleasant adventure had fairly killed all chance of sleep for that night, so after our trio of friends had lighted their pipes, Kenyon drew Leigh and Grenville on one side out of earshot of the rest of the party. "And now," said he, "let us seriously consider our position, for it is one of very great danger; but first, give me your attention, Leigh, whilst I fulfil my promise and relate to you the history of Zero so far as it is known to me, after which your cousin will doubtless cap my information with a few interesting and instructive details regarding the life and opinions of the greatest scoundrel on the face of the earth.

"Zero, whose real name by the way is Monckton Bassett, is, I am ashamed to admit, an American by birth, and hails from New York, where his father originally figured as a respectable and a fairly successful foreign merchant. Master Bassett was an only and a precocious child, and having at the early age of twenty-three succeeded in breaking his poor mother's heart by the wild

50

wickedness of his ways, and ruining his foolishly indulgent father by wheedling him into bearing from time to time the expense of a systematic and unsuccessful gambling career, next threw in his lot with a villainous card-sharper named Weston Harper, through whose instrumentality he first came under the notice of the police, being, as I proved at the time, very nearly concerned in a burglary committed upon the house of a wealthy New Yorker, to whose daughter he had formerly been engaged. This gentleman, however, Mr. Harmsworth by name, had abruptly put a stop to the embryo love affair when he accidentally learned the life that his would-be son-in-law was leading. The burglary was not the worst of it; for Mr. Harmsworth was deliberately and unnecessarily shot dead in his bed, and there was every reason to believe that young Bassett's hand had fired the fatal shot, though I could never absolutely bring the murder home to him. However, we fixed the burglary on this precious pair, and both got a ten-years' sentence, but escaped by bribing the gaolers, and successfully made their way to Salt Lake City, after which, like a fool, I ceased to bother my head about them. This was six years ago you see," added Kenyon, "and I wasn't quite so well posted in the ways of criminals as I am now supposed to be. Well, gentlemen, about a couple of years after this I myself became affianced to a sweet young girl named Roxana Kenyon, my own cousin on the father's side; and, as I was rapidly rising in my new profession, we had every prospect of being united at no distant date; but, to save time, I had better carry my story forward another two years--that is, bringing it to the year 1879, when our wedding-day was fixed for the 15th of April. Our house was taken and furnished throughout, and everything was duly arranged; but, on the night before the wedding, my bride disappeared as completely as if the very earth had opened and swallowed her." For a moment the stern detective faltered, and, overcome by his conflicting emotions, buried his face in his bands, quickly, however, recovering himself and continuing his story. "There," he said impatiently, "it was all over, and the rest is soon told. On Roxana's bed, which had not been slept in, I discovered a scrap of white paper with a dead black circle skilfully drawn upon it--exactly similar, let me remark, to that hieroglyphic found upon the body of the late Lady Drelincourt, only that in my case, upon the reverse side of the paper, there appeared the words: Zero gets even with Stanforth Kenyon over the Harmsworth burglary.' I knew the writing well, and the hand that wrote it was the hand of Monckton Bassett. Without loss of time, I beat up his career subsequent to the burglary and prior to the abduction, and discovered through trusted agents that he had been absent from the New World for nearly three years, and after having returned to Utah, possessed of considerable property and accompanied by the woman he calls his wife, had again gone abroad, and was then believed to be somewhere in South Africa engaged upon business connected with the community of the Latter Day Saints.

"I at once sent in my resignation to the Chief of Police, who, however, refused to accept it, giving me instead a three years' holiday to prosecute my search, as well as many kindly offers of assistance both monetary and official. Declining the former, I sailed for Cape Town as soon as ever I could possibly get away, and finally worked round to Durban, where, in a lucky moment for all of us, I tumbled up against Leigh's advertisement, and, recognising in Driffield an old friend of mine, professional instinct prompted me to call and pump him with regard to Grenville the missing; but it was only after the lawyer had made me a most generous offer with the object of inducing me to lead a search party into the Interior, and had given me the history of the adventures of you two in East Utah, that a sudden inspiration gave me the clue to Monckton Bassett's whereabouts.

"Zero, I said to myself, means just nothing at all: why then has this man--who, by the way, thinks no small beer of himself--adopted such an extraordinary name?

"Next, is there any place or district in Africa bearing the name of Zero. No! Stop! then like a living ray of light upon my mental darkness was flashed the answer--the Line--the Equatorial Line--Number Nought-- that is Zero. I wired New York at once, obtained the latest particulars of his known movements, and then, with complete faith in my good angel, I shut up my notebook, went right off to Driffield and engaged myself in the search both body and soul. And now, my friends, I am here, and you, Grenville, are free, and all I ask is that you will both wait long enough for me to settle my little account with this infernal scoundrel, and then Westward Ho for all of us."

"One moment, Kenyon," interjected Leigh; "I claim this fiend from hell as my personal property. Think, man, you have but lost one who, it is true, was almost your wife; but I, ah! God, he owes me everything-- wife, child, my love, my life--my very trust in Heaven, and for this I hold my right to prove upon his vile body to be before the right of any living man;" and, strung to the highest pitch, by the very worst and strongest passions of human nature, these two firm friends fairly glared at one another in the thoughtless anger of this intense moment.

"Peace, gentlemen," said the attentive Grenville, "peace! Remember I too have a right to act in this matter, if aught of wrong received upon this earth can give the right of revenge upon a fellow-man. Nay, Alf, I am not seeking to enforce my claim. God's hand rests upon this curse of Central Africa, as I told him to his face, and when his time comes he must go even as we; yet do I fervently pray that one of ourselves may be the fleshly instrument selected to cause his going.

"And now, Kenyon, how called you your affianced wife?--Roxana, was it not?--Roxana--ay, an Asiatic name signifying, if I mistake not, the `Goddess of the Morning.' It must be the same--hear me out, old fellow," as Kenyon rose, fairly trembling with excitement. "A young white woman, known amongst the natives by a name signifying `The Star of the Morning,' and reputed to be very fair to look upon, was brought over from Madagascar to Zanzibar by Zero and his so-called wife, and was a prisoner in their hands until just before the time that I and my men were taken captives by his band. He was then working his way up here from the coast--but during his absence from camp one day, his zareeba was stormed by a horde of Arabs, who swept out the best half of his property, including the white girl and upwards of one hundred repeating-rifles, the latter having been purchased and carefully smuggled in for the use of his men.

"When Zero returned, he behaved, I heard, like a creature bereft of his senses; he had, of course, expected to make `big money' out of the sale of the girl, and to reduce the Arabs themselves with the Winchesters, whereas the boot was now very much on the other leg. I also heard that he cautiously followed the tracks of the spoilers, but found that the girl had persuaded them to take her to Zanzibar, where she was quickly liberated through the kind agency of the British Consul, and was supposed to have left for America. Zero then made tracks for home, and came upon our hunting party in an evil hour, and the rest you know."

Kenyon gripped Grenville's hand in silence, and the tears chased one another rapidly down his cheeks. "God bless you, old fellow," he blurted out at last: "it was well worth saving your life, if only for this--I was fast becoming a brute, and you've given me back love and hope, and with them my faith in Heaven." Grenville and his cousin rose quietly and left him alone with the cruel memories of the darksome past and the bright hopes of the near future, and nothing in all their lives became them better; but as they walked away Leigh put his hand on his cousin's shoulder: "Good old Dick," he said, in a tone of anguish, "you have no hope nor help for me." Then his voice changing to a positive hiss--"You may talk till you're black in the face, my boy, but I'll never leave this spot until I've sent back yonder cursed scoundrel to the hell from whence he came."

Before Grenville could answer, however, Kenyon called to the twain to return, and, sitting down again, Grenville gave his companions a pretty full account of the abominable cruelties of Zero and his "wife," and of the way they were devastating the country in almost every direction; and Kenyon now learnt, to his surprise, that an enormous slave-trade was done in the very heart of Africa, and that so far from trafficking in "Black Ivory" direct with the Coast, either east or west, the slavers' market for human flesh and blood was found principally amongst tribes which lay to the west of Equatoria, and as the purchase money-- when not provided in ivory--usually consisted of pure rock-gold or gold-dust packed in quills, the slaves were in all probability passed on to Dahomey or Asyanti, whence they no doubt gravitated northwards and ultimately found their way to Morocco, travelling incredible distances and constantly changing hands.

Towards the rising sun Master Zero's operations were of a restricted, and, to him, an extremely unsatisfactory nature, as his position was everywhere hemmed in by hostile Arabs, who kept with a strong hand the country they had originally secured by artifice, and to whom, as followers of "the one True Prophet," Zero was doubly hateful, on account of his Mormon connections.

The man was himself absent at the present time, personally conducting an important "slave-drive," but might be expected back in the course of two or three days, when the whole of his captives would be passed on to the native King, whom the slavers were now busily entertaining, and who was, in fact, simply waiting for Zero's return to "make his trade" and march westward with his purchases; and until this matter was satisfactorily disposed of, Grenville was inclined to believe that no serious attempt would be made to interfere with themselves, but once let this fiend in human form get clear of the pressing business in hand, and he would promptly turn his attention to their own little account and would give them no rest until the affair was settled, one way or the other.

Chapter 9: The War Trail

As the question had now purely resolved into one of warfare, offensive or defensive, Amaxosa was called into council, in order that a definite and feasible plan of action might be formulated.

Leigh and Kenyon were disposed to stay just where they were, as the place seemed well-adapted for defence, had an ample supply of water, and was, at the same time, sufficiently close to Equatoria to be handy in the event of their party finding it desirable to sally out upon Zero's position.

Grenville, however, was distrustful with regard to the cave itself, as he half-suspected that Muzi Zimba the hermit had a secret method of entering the Mormon Town without going all round by the forest; and if such a way existed, Zero would be quite certain to know of it, although his followers might be kept, in ignorance for a purpose; and, of course, it would never do for our friends to get themselves fixed between two fires.

The Zulu chief listened intently to all the arguments pro and con, but never opened his mouth until Grenville, addressing him in the Zulu tongue, asked him to express his opinion upon the matter under notice.

"Can my father," he said, "tell his son Amaxosa, whither the Black One (Zero) has journeyed?"

"Surely, my brother," answered Grenville, "didst thou not hear when but yesterday we stood yonder tethered like oxen for the slaughter that he had compassed thrice three days' travel towards the east, and that his bloodhounds could not return in time to gnaw the flesh from our broken bones?"

"Ay, Inkoos," was the reply, "I heard the words, but yet believed them not. Hearken! my father, when the Black One went forth, he went at dead of night, and with him went the savage dogs and but one hundred men with guns. Think, then, my father, for well thou knowest that did the Black One journey but one day towards the rising sun without a full impi at his back, he would be eaten up by the Arab tribes, who dwell outside this land of witchcraft, and who hate him even as we do. More, my father, I know that the men lied when they spoke, for only yester morn did I see two of the snow-white message birds arrive, and they came from the mountains of the distant southern lands.

"Hearken to my words, oh, chiefs! If ye follow them, doubt not that all shall yet go well.

"To-morrow night, when the moon rises, will the Black One rest beneath the cool shadow of yon distant peak; let us be there, oh! chiefs, and he shall sleep the sleep that never wakes in life.

"Thus shall the matter go--thou knowest well the place, my father--the evil ones will come in from the southern lands--the Lands of Lakes and Rivers--and will set their kraal beneath the great white mountain, and towards the setting sun, at the spot in the deep hollow where there ever flows a spring of clear, sweet water, where is a mighty wall of rock on this side and on that side, and a hill hard to be climbed towards the further north; and it shall be, my father, that when the evil ones, filled with food and worn with the toil of the day, have entered into the trap, and have lain them down to rest, that we will turn from its course the flowing waters of the great river which runs on the path of the rising sun, and will fill the place with weeping, and with the bodies of dead men.

"With ten of these low black fellows (Zanzibaris) will I turn the river, and with those that remain, and with the spears and guns, shalt thou, my father, safely keep the northern hill, and it shall be that ere the arrows of the dawn glance upon the snows of the great white mountain, the evil ones shall be stamped flat and eaten up, and the foul carcase of the Black Master of Evil himself, shall be but food for the vultures and the wolves. I have spoken."

The Zulu's idea was, unquestionably, a very fine one, and promised to rid our friends of their arch-enemy, together with a hundred of the very vilest of his following at one fell swoop, and it was therefore determined that the plan should be adopted in its entirety, their own party thus taking the initiative.

If the scheme failed, the little band would be really no worse off than they were at the present time, whilst if it succeeded--and with the cunning of the Zulu at its back, it certainly had every chance of success--the campaign would be capitally inaugurated by drawing the lion's teeth at the very first attempt. Zero, it was conceded upon all sides, was the one man to be feared, and could they but dispose of him out of hand, the Mormon-cum-Slaver fraternity would be like a ship without a helm, and would very soon find itself in unpleasantly rough water.

Our friends calculated that the slavers, on discovering the near approach of the water, would first drive their black captives up the hill, and after Grenville's party had allowed these to pass and save themselves, his men would keep the road against the slavers and fiercely contest the narrow passage hand to hand, with axe and spear, rifle and pistol. It would be a stubborn fight; that was certain, for, granting that the slavers had expended a few men on their distant foray, they would still be in the proportion of two to one; and if they once penetrated the ranks of our friends, it would be all up with the little band, as they would instantly be driven back by sheer weight of numbers, into a ready-made watery grave of their own providing.

At dawn, therefore, the entire party breakfasted hastily, and, after leaving in the outer cave a few articles likely to be of service to the friendly old hermit, made their way quickly down the hill, and striking well into the fog-banks at its foot, steered a straight course for the distant mountains; Grenville and the other rescued white men, who were extremely feeble, being carried by the Zanzibaris in hammocks, so as to husband, as far as possible, what little strength they possessed.

The Zulu knew his ground thoroughly, and ere the mist had been completely sucked up by the sun, had got his followers some miles on their way, and travelling smoothly along the shallow bed of a small stream, whose overhanging banks provided a capital safeguard against prying eyes.

Naught of interest occurred that day, and by keeping the men hard at it, so as to shorten the next day's journey, a good forty miles was knocked off before the tired wayfarers lay down to snatch a brief spell of rest until the tardy appearance of the moon provided them with sufficient light to proceed by, when the little band again took the road and kept moving until the waning light put a welcome period to their labours, and sleeping a heavy, dreamless sleep until the sun once more awoke them to the weary toil and travel of another burning tropic day.

A glorious sight now met the wondering eyes of our friends, for right before them and distant perhaps a score of miles across the veldt, rose the giant fabric of the wished-for mountain, now sharply defined in every detail of its vast and massive grandeur. Straight up into the very heavens themselves shot one glorious, glittering peak, whose perfect beauty was beyond all earthly praise: around its lofty summit the everlasting snows had grouped themselves like gleaming, flashing jewels in the radiant crown of this mighty cloud-clad monarch of the equator. Wreaths of filmy, fleecy mist drifted slowly here and there across his distorted shoulders, which were seamed in every direction with yawning fissures, whose awful blackness was rendered even more striking by contrast with the unmatched, glittering glory of this solitary inland peak, whilst the green and rolling veldt, sweeping away unbroken to the horizon on every hand, formed a fit setting for this lovely, lonely diadem of God's own fashioning.

Soon, however, the heat-clouds settled down upon the mountain, veiling from sight all but its lower vast proportions, upon whose rugged sides no vestige of vegetation could as yet be seen.

With but a short rest at mid-day, our adventurers pressed on, in spite of the stifling heat, and reached the spring of which Amaxosa had spoken, about three o'clock in the afternoon, when the fighting brigade instantly threw themselves down to rest and sleep in the grateful shade cast by the giant walls of overhanging rock, which stretched grimly upwards on either hand, their barren wildness relieved only here and there by a few odd patches of trees and bush.

Grenville himself kept guard, and Kenyon at once proceeded down the pass and climbed some way up the mountain side to keep a sharp look-out over the southern veldt, whilst Leigh and Amaxosa turned their faces towards the river, and closely scrutinised its banks for quite half a mile beyond the further exit of the pass ere they discovered a species of creek, or inlet, only two score yards from the edge of the track, and in every way eminently suited to their requirements. Leigh then returned to the spring, and promptly dispatched ten of the Zanzibaris, with their implements, to join the Zulu chief, and to lie hidden until they received his further orders.

The scheme, artfully as it hod been planned, had one weak spot in it, which gave both Grenville and Kenyon much serious thought, and that anxiety was caused by the certain knowledge that Zero had with him his three magnificent bloodhounds, which, token in conjunction with their vile master--who was, perhaps, more of a brute than the noble animals themselves--composed the most formidable quartette in Equatoria. Grenville had already warned his friends not to waste their bullets on the dogs, but to leave the brutes to him, as should the slavers once get within range, he would not raise a hand against them until he had first settled with the canine element His great fear was, however, that the hounds would warn their masters of the presence of the little band the moment they struck the scent. The way through the pass being, however, mostly composed of rock, and a heavy gang of slaves going on in front, it was, of course, more than possible that the scent would be rendered too faint to attract anything but a mere passing whimper from the great dogs.

When the party had had perhaps three hours' rest, a shrill whistle was suddenly heard from Kenyon, and looking upwards Grenville saw him making the agreed danger signal.

Half-an-hour later the American rejoined his friends, and reported that a vast mob of human beings had come within range of his field-glass during the last hour, and were now a score of miles away and heading direct for their own position in the pass. News was quickly sent round to Amaxosa, who, however, soon appeared and carried off the chief, who, next to himself, stood highest among his own men. Him he carefully inducted into the mysteries of the "Zulu irrigation scheme," as Kenyon styled it, and then returned to the main body, where he considered "his father would need his arm"--the fact, of course, being, that the splendid fellow was simply spoiling for a good fight with his late tormentors.

Chapter 10: No Quarter

Hardly had our friends perfected the details of their scheme for surprising the slavers, than darkness rushed upon them like a tangible thing. All, however, were much too excited to sleep, and, as soon as the rising moon gave sufficient light, the whole party removed itself beyond the steep crest of the northern hill, and impatiently awaited developments, or, as the Zulus have it, "fought the fight of sit down."

It had been agreed amongst them, that the slavers were to have a clear hour allowed them from the time of entering the pass, to permit of their settling down quietly for the night, and this hour would of course, be employed to advantage by the men in charge of the "water department," whilst the defenders of the hill had of necessity to take their cue from the movements of the enemy as occasion might arise.

For once in a way, matters fell out even better than the most sanguine had dared to hope. The slavers trooped quietly in, the dogs failing to show the slightest sign of uneasiness, and as soon as the slaves had been watered at the spring, the wretched creatures, to the number of about three hundred, all carefully manacled, were mercilessly driven on towards Equatoria, guarded by half a score of heavily-armed and powerful-looking ruffians, whilst Zero and the rest of his following encamped for the night beside the spring, taking no precautions whatever against surprise, and obviously considering themselves perfectly safe in their own happy hunting-grounds, relying, no doubt, upon the dogs to give them timely notice of any hostile approach. Nothing could have been better than this arrangement; for had the miserable slaves been detained in the hollow of the pass, it would have caused our friends very considerable difficulty to separate the poor unoffending creatures, from their sworn vengeance upon Zero and his host of scoundrels, whereas now, every shot would have a definite and decided aim.

After the dismal procession had filed out of sight, the time hung very heavily on the hands of the anxious watchers on the hill, and none seemed to feel it more keenly than did Leigh. He fidgeted first with his rifle, and then with his revolvers, until Grenville and Kenyon made sure that one or other of the weapons would explode, and prematurely unmask the whole affair, when matters would in all likelihood get uncomfortably warm for their little party.

Leigh was possessed of but one desire, and that was to get sight of Zero, when none who watched his face as Grenville did, could doubt that there would be bloodshed.

Slowly an hour dragged out its weary length. Below all was still as death, the slavers were fast asleep round their fire, and as a gentle zephyr was breezing in from the south, there was no scent to disturb the repose of the great dogs, who seemed to appreciate the warmth of the fire, equally with their tired masters.

All at once the death-like silence was rent by a thundering explosion, which seemed to fairly shake the mighty fabric of the mountain, and to rend the very vault of heaven itself, whilst in the twinkling of an eye, every man amongst the slavers was on his feet, gun in hand, and gazing inquiringly at his nearest comrade.

Hardly had the Titanic echoes ceased to answer one another amongst the mountain fastnesses, than a wild cry went up from the wretched men beside the spring, as they saw the angry river come foaming and dancing towards them--a frothing, bubbling sea of glancing foam--as it flew along down the narrow pass under the weird rays of the ivory moonlight.

But a single look the slavers gave; then, turning as one man, the whole band rushed blindly for the hill, but scarcely had they commenced to climb, when the crown of the ascent seemed to fairly open before their astonished eyes in a glancing sheet of flame, as Grenville gave the word, and two score angry rifles poured their deadly contents into the surging mob of humanity but fifty yards below, whilst a chorus of shrieks and imprecations went up to heaven, and men rolled over in every direction, dead and dying, thus testifying to the fatal results of the discharge.

The slavers paused aghast; but, with a wild, deep-throated bay, the noble hounds sprang forward, undaunted by the presence of the foe-- useless bravery, for Grenville kept his word: the moonlight was good enough to shoot by, and three shots from his Winchester accounted for the three great dogs in much less time than it takes to tell.

Meantime the water was rushing forward like a living thing, and the slavers, forced onwards by it, dashed up the hill in a positive frenzy of fear, paying no attention to their leader, who vainly shouted to them to keep their heads, as the water would take some time to rise the height of the steep ascent. On they came in spite of another blinding discharge, which absolutely singed their faces and thinned their ranks by quite one-half, and then, hand to hand, the combatants met with a mighty roar. Hither and thither swung the fight in all its ghastly details, the crash of the axes, and the rapid detonations of the revolver-pistols; almost drowning the war-cries of the Zulus as they wreaked their righteous vengeance upon their late tormentors. Soon, however, friend and foe were so closely blent together that even Grenville--who kept out of a scrimmage in which he was yet too weak to take his accustomed part--found it extremely difficult work to get in a single shot without danger to his own people.

The Slaver-Chief was unquestionably a brave man, and in his fighting cry there was inspiration for his band; but what could he do when three such men as Leigh, Kenyon, and Amaxosa would, if they could help it, fight neither with small nor great but with himself only; whilst Grenville, meantime, watched, lynx-eyed, for a chance of putting a bullet through him?

Four times did this determined trio charge the slavers, axe in hand, and Zero himself at last fell upon a heap of his companions, whose living bodies had lately been his only rampart against these vindictive and invincible foes.

Upon the fall of the Slaver-Chief a mighty shout went up from the little band of friends, and the few remaining slavers immediately threw down their arms and begged for mercy. Mercy! Fools! What could they expect? A Zulu shows no mercy to a beaten foe, and if beaten himself he asks none. Moreover, the foe in this case richly deserved all he got, for he had been guilty of every species of senseless and abominable cruelty under heaven, and merited to the full a far more dreadfully retributive justice than the sudden and almost painless death which he received at the hands of his relentless executioners.

So much for one side, now for the other. Four of the white men rescued from the Mormons by Leigh and Kenyon, were stone dead, as were three Zanzibaris, who had stayed on the spot in an unaccustomed and ill-fated excess of valour or curiosity. The remaining white man, a sturdy young Highlander, named Duncan Ewan, had received a nasty scalp wound, whilst five of the Zulus were lying about very severely cut up, though all would recover with careful treatment. Of the three champions, Amaxosa was the only one who had received any hurt, and that was superficial, a bullet having grazed and laid open one side of his face. Hastily our friends shook hands with one another--and with themselves, so to speak-- and then Leigh and Amaxosa, supported by all the available Zulus, started off at speed upon the trail of the departed slave-gang, leaving Grenville and Kenyon (together with the frightened Zanzibaris, who were cautiously returning by twos and threes from the four winds of heaven, whither they had fled when the first shot was fired) to get the wounded into a place of safety; for the water was still rapidly rising, and once over the crest of the hill, it would simply sweep the whole plain towards the north, unless something could be done to stop its wild career. Quickly getting the wounded men out of the pass, and some little way up the mountain side, Grenville and Kenyon next made a careful examination of the old course, of the river beyond the pass, and found that if they could blow up one mighty piece of rock, the river would immediately descend through the medium of a waterfall into its own original bed. The pair, accordingly, returned to the scene of the fight in order to collect all the gunpowder belonging to the deceased slavers; but hardly had they reached the spot than Kenyon, to Grenville's utter astonishment, let out a bitter curse. "Fooled," he cried, "as I'm a living sinner--fooled again by that cursed fox!" and turning quickly, as a mocking laugh grated upon their ears, Zero was seen by the pair standing upon a rock at the northern outlet of the pass, perhaps a hundred yards away, and taking aim at them with his rifle. Grenville's Winchester went up like a flash, and the two reports blended into one. The slaver's bullet whistled harmlessly past their ears, and at the same instant he was seen to drop his gun, and clap his hand upon his left shoulder, and then, shaking his fist angrily at Grenville, he hurled a vile curse at the two friends, and, springing down from the rock, was at once lost to view amidst the gloomy shadows of the mountain.

Whilst Grenville collected the powder, Kenyon promptly set out in pursuit of the slaver, but could find no trace of his whereabouts. The fellow's claws were, however, cut for the nonce, as there was blood upon the rock where he had been standing, and his rifle was still lying there, the hammer having been cut clean away by Grenville's bullet. So that wounded, unarmed, and unsupported, it was a shrewd count that they would easily get him when daylight came, and get him they must, for he clearly was a dangerous, as well as a very slippery, villain.

Our friends soon succeeded in blowing up the rock, and preparing a new outlet for the water, and this was not accomplished any too soon, as by the time they had collected the arms, which were everywhere strewed about the confined field of battle, the water was already lapping gently against the upper edges of the steep ascent, and in another ten minutes it was racing down the track, and shooting clear over the beetling wall of rock, thus returning to its own natural bed in the shape of a magnificent waterfall, whose enormous volume, as it fell, waked a mighty echo, which would henceforward cause a perpetual and thundering murmur amongst the rocky glens of the mountains, as if nature were herself complaining of this irremediable mischief, wrought by the puny hand of careless and unthinking man.

Hardly had Grenville and Kenyon regained the mountain side, than the report of firearms was heard away across the veldt, and the quick flashes of Leigh's repeating-rifle could be distinctly seen. In a few short minutes all was again as quiet as death, and the twain looked anxiously at one another, yearning to know with whom the victory rested, when all at once, through the still night air, and right across the rolling veldt was wafted the wild war-cry of the children of the Undi, proclaiming the successful accomplishment of another act of retribution, and the absolutely triumphant success of Amaxosa's daring scheme for the destruction of the foe--a success which was marred only by the single detail of the temporary escape from their vengeance, of the Slaver-Chief himself.

Grenville and Kenyon next lighted a large fire to apprise the detachment out upon the veldt, of the exact position of the party upon the mountain side; and this having been done, Kenyon, who never travelled without a complete surgeon's "kit," proceeded to attend to the injuries of the wounded men, and soon had the poor fellows as comfortable as circumstances permitted.

Shortly after this, the Zulu, Umbulanzi, in charge of the "water department," and to whom belonged no small share of the credit of this successful affair, made his appearance, accompanied by all but two of the Zanzibaris, who, under his direction, had acted in the capacity of sappers.

It seemed that Amaxosa had fortunately foreseen the possibility of this detachment hitting upon a bed of rock, and thus having their work stopped, and the whole scheme completely ruined, and he had, therefore, supplied his confrere with a 56 pound keg of powder out of Leigh's ample stores, and finding that a great slab of broken ironstone rock was spoiling his little game, this Zulu had coolly slapped the whole keg under the edge of this obstruction, and blown the entire affair sky-high, and along with it two of the Zanzibaris, whose unfortunate curiosity had prevailed over their accustomed discretion.

"Haow Inkoos," he said, speaking rapidly to Grenville in the Zulu tongue, "it was indeed a very great sight, and never will Umbulanzi see the like again. The rock shot up to the heavens on high, and with it went the low black fellows. The great stone came down again, my father; but, though I waited long for the low fellows, they came not, and as the cowards must have run away for good, Umbulanzi did not stay."

The moon was waning fast, but the stars still held the curtains of night over the wide-stretched whispering veldt, when the victorious party of Amaxosa, accompanied by the slave-gang, was heard approaching from the north, and upon their arrival it was found that the little band had not suffered further in any way, having satisfactorily "rushed" the remaining slavers, and disposed of them every one.

The anger of Leigh and Amaxosa, however, knew no bounds when the cunning escape of the arch-enemy was made known to them, and both bitterly repented that they had not made sure of the fox by knocking him on the head, and registered a solemn vow to commit no further mistakes of the kind, should Zero fall into their hands again. Clearly, however, nothing could be done until dawn of day, and it was decided, therefore, to let the rescued slaves sleep in their irons, and to wait for daylight, in order that their captors might gain some little insight into the character of their new charges. So, having set a watch of Zanzibaris, overlooked by Grenville himself, the tired army laid itself down, and was soon fast asleep, whilst the rescued slaves, who had been told the good news that they would be liberated in the morning, chattered to one another throughout the livelong night, like a troop of monkeys in the forest. With the first gleam of daylight, Leigh and Amaxosa were afoot, and without even staying to dispatch a mouthful of food, threw themselves upon the bloodstained trail of the Slaver-Chief, and were almost instantly lost to sight amongst the dense fog-banks which overhung the surrounding veldt in every direction.

Chapter 11: The People of the Stick

First thing in the morning the slaves were unshackled, and, after all had breakfasted, they were interviewed through the medium of one of the native "guides," and our friends found to their horror that Zero and his band of fiends had fallen upon this people, in the night, and after picking out 300 of the finest among the men, had effectually stamped out the remainder of the tribe, both root and branch, by fastening them all, young men and maidens, old men and children, in their huts, and then setting fire to the village , lining the palisades with their rifles meantime, lest any should break out and escape, to bring down upon the murderers swift and unsparing vengeance at the hands of a great and warlike native people, who lived near at hand, and who were closely related to the stricken tribe.

They seemed an intelligent and brave people, and would no doubt have given a good account of themselves if Zero had not taken them utterly unawares in their huts by night; and the men, who were as a rule fine, athletic-looking fellows, declared that they would follow the white men to the death, if they would but lead their party on and entirely eat up these slavers, whom they denounced as monsters of cruelty--one man stating that the great bloodhounds had been deliberately fed by Zero himself with the flesh of several baby boys, who had been roasted alive, and he added that, if the white men would not go with them, his own people would carry on the war, even if they had to fight with empty hands.

This was so far good, but our friends were utterly at their wits' end regarding arms for their new allies, who clearly did not understand the use of guns, whilst the few spears and axes saved from the slavers deceased in the fight of the previous day, would not equip one-fourth of their number.

On being asked, however, what weapons they would prefer to use, the men replied proudly that they were called "Atagbondo" or "the People of the Stick," in consequence of their habit of fighting only with long-handled clubs, which they could cut for themselves as soon as forest land, similar to their own, was reached by the party.

These clubs, it appeared, formed their sole weapon of offence, but they also used--as our friends found at a later date--an instrument of a most peculiar nature, and of which their white leaders could not at first comprehend the utility.

The instrument referred to, was a neatly-fashioned piece of extremely hard wood, from a yard to a yard and a half in length, thick in the centre, where it contained a cavity to protect the hand, and tapering to both of its slender-looking extremities. At its widest part it was but some few inches broad, was fitted with a thong in which to slip the hand, and generally gave one the idea of a modified quarter-staff with an elongated bulb in the middle. The instrument was called a "quayre;" and when this people went into battle the warriors tapped the quayre against the shaft of the club and produced a rattling volume of sound, which could be heard a mile away, and was supposed to strike terror into the heart of the foe; whilst the quayre itself, which they handled in a most expert fashion, was used not only to ward off blows struck at the persons of the men with native axes, clubs, or similar weapons, but even in parrying spear-thrusts--a difficult operation, which they performed, however, with no little dexterity, whilst the quayre was at the same time less than one-third of the weight of a very ordinary fighting shield.

On being informed that the white men were about to hold a council of war, and would like them to be represented, the chief of the Atagbondo stepped forward. Probably forty years of age, this man was a magnificent specimen of his race, who are all very much above the average height of Englishmen. He stood, probably, six feet two inches, but whilst he was not quite so tall as Amaxosa he possessed a more heavily built frame, being broader and deeper in the chest, and more massive in his appearance generally. Taken all through, he was, perhaps, the more powerful of the two men, but what the Zulu lacked in point of muscle was more than compensated for by the symmetry of his build, and his consequently superior activity; besides, this was relatively speaking, a man of peace, whilst the fierce Zulu was a man of war from his youth up, trained in every art and artifice, and inured to hardships and dangers by the experiences of many a well-fought field.

The Chieftain of the Stick had an intensely "Negro" face, but without its ordinary stolidity, and, in common with his warriors, had his head shaved with the exception of a sort of central tuft, which somewhat resembled the "scalp lock" of the North American Indians, and through this tuft was thrust, in the case of every man, a miniature quayre, beautifully carved in ivory, standing, in point of fact, for the "totem" of his tribe, and proudly indicating the race from which he sprang.

The chief--whose name, by the way, was "Barad," or "The Hailstorm"--in a few well-chosen words, thanked the white men for releasing himself and his people, and then declared his intention of putting his party entirely into the hands of our friends, until vengeance had been taken upon the wicked men "who dwelt on the frontier of the far north, and amongst the mountains of Muzi Zimba the Ancient." Our friends were more than surprised to find that their new allies both knew and reverenced the friendly hermit who overlooked Zero's location, but found that beyond sending the old man a yearly "hongo," or tribute, they knew nothing of him, but regarded him as a "very big fetish."

Amaxosa and Leigh now returning empty-handed and disgusted from their search after Zero, a council was called to receive their report. This was as short as it was unsatisfactory. The slaver had been unquestionably wounded by Grenville's bullet, but it was, unfortunately, one of those wounds which act upon a flying foe as they do upon a running deer, and simply make him leap the faster.

The pair had followed the track of the fugitive for close upon ten miles, beyond which it was useless to go, as they now knew positively from the "sign" that Zero had unearthed a canoe from its hiding-place amongst some rocks near the river, and had gone off downstream, and was, therefore, completely out of reach for the time being.

Smarting with fury at the crushing defeat he had sustained, and maddened by the loss of both friends and plunder, the party might safely reckon upon the slaver delivering a crushing attack upon their position at no distant date, and it only now became a question as to whether they were sufficiently strong to go out and meet him in the open, or had better choose out a likely place on the mountain side, and make it good, until the loss on the side of the foe provided them with a chance of wiping him out "one time," as the natives say, with a well-delivered sortie.

True, the little band had now the not-to-be-despised support of three hundred able-bodied men, all thirsting for vengeance upon the common foe; but then, these men were entirely unarmed, whilst Zero, besides mustering close upon a thousand of his own rogues, well supplied with guns, would in all probability be supported by the native King already referred to, backed by several thousands of his followers, all armed with bow and spear, in the use of which they were said to be both bold and skilful.

Ultimately, therefore, our friends decided to stay where they were, or, rather,

68

to select a strong position on the mountain capable of a sustained defence, and in the interval which they might calculate upon prior to an attack, they determined to employ themselves in an endeavour to arm, after their own peculiar fashion, the warlike People of the Stick, and to induct the most intelligent amongst them into the mysteries of the rifle. This last would necessitate some little expenditure in the way of ammunition; but, as the party had abundance of powder taken from the vanquished slavers, they were fortunately in a position to afford this outlay.

Towards evening, the indefatigable Amaxosa, who had gone out on a tour of inspection, returned with an exceptionally favourable report, and the first thing on the morrow the whole band removed to the rocky fastness selected for their occupation by the keen-eyed Zulu chief, and all hands were at once set to work to excavate, to build earthworks, and in many other ways to amplify the already considerable natural defences of the place, whilst the Atagbondo flayed every bush and tree within a scoro of miles, to furnish themselves with offensive clubs and defensive quayres.

Chapter 12: Fighting the Flames

For fully three days did our friends occupy themselves in the very necessary work of perfecting the defences of their stronghold on the mountain, and in teaching a picked dozen of the Atagbondo the use of the rifle, with which weapon they soon became fair marksmen, in the native acceptance of the term.

On the fourth day, however, a discovery, trifling in itself, convinced the party that, so far from having been forgotten by Zero, they were at present occupying the whole of his earnest attention.

The incident in question was the accidental notice taken by Kenyon of a small bird wheeling round and round their position; closer and closer it came, until all could see perfectly well that it was a white carrier pigeon, bearing a message. Finding, however, that the party did not whistle it in, the bird grew shy, and quickly took to flight Leigh raised his rifle with the intention of bringing it down, but Kenyon stopped him just in time.

"Don't shoot, old fellow," he said; "I've a fancy to let that bird severely alone. I want to know just where it's bound for at the present moment."

Watching very carefully, the pigeon was at last seen to enter a clump of bush about half a mile up the mountain side, and scarcely ten minutes later, either it, or a similar bird, left the same cover, and winged its rapid way due north.

The inference was plain, and our friends looked blankly at one another; but, ere they could speak, the Zulu chief had summoned Umbulanzi and directed him to take two men, thoroughly search the suspected spot, and put to the assegai anyone they might find lurking there.

Grenville and Kenyon would have much preferred taking the spy--if spy there was--alive, but the fear that his presence would cause the injured People of the Stick to overstep all restraint and become guilty of some fearful act of barbaric cruelty, decided them to let the man fight it out to the bitter end for his own life, rather than to permit him to fall into the hands of a raging mob of naked savages, whose tenderest mercies, maddened as they were by their frightful wrongs, would be cruel indeed.

Anxiously our friends watched the progress of the three Zulus up the mountain, and all at once Leigh took a fancy to follow them, and was soon swinging up the slant with rapid steps, accompanied by Amaxosa and Kenyon.

The Zulus reached the spot and plunged into the cover, from which there instantly arose a tremendous hubbub, and a moment later all three reappeared, fairly driven out by half a score of white men, and fighting furiously with their spears against several of the slavers, who were armed with axes, whilst the remainder stood by eagerly seeking an opportunity to use their guns.

Promptly Leigh and Kenyon pitched forward their rifles, and two of the slavers instantly rolled head over heels down the mountain side, whilst at the same moment, uttering a wild shout of encouragement, Amaxosa dashed forward like an arrow from the bow, and in another second was side by side with his warriors, their nervous arms dealing out death and disaster with every sweeping blow. When Leigh and Kenyon reached the platform upon which this tragedy had been enacted, there was but one of the enemy left alive, and he was engaged in a terrific hand-to-hand combat with Amaxosa. All at once the Zulu's axe broke off short in the haft, and the ruffian slaver rushed at him with a victorious shout. Springing lightly to one side, however, the active chief easily avoided the deadly stroke aimed at him by his opponent, whom he seized the next instant from behind, with his powerful hands pinning the man's arms to his side, and before anyone could interfere, or even speak, with one mighty effort the fierce Zulu fairly swung his hapless foe from the ground, and then dashed him down full upon the rock, on his bare skull, which was crushed in like an egg-shell, the awful blow, of course, killing him on the spot, and an instant later the mountain side echoed to the triumphant notes of the famous Undi war-chant.

"Oh, my father," said the great Zulu, contemplating his handiwork with satisfaction, and speaking to Leigh, "it was a great fight; few could have slain the man with empty hands. Sleep softly, ye evildoers; the Lion of the Undi bids you sleep!"

Carefully examining the cover from which the discomfited foe had sprung, our friends found that it consisted of a shallow cave in the face of the rock, the entrance being masked by low bushes, and a thick undergrowth of wild vines. In this hiding-place Kenyon discovered a basket containing three white and two black pigeons, whilst a note, evidently the one just received, lay upon the rocky floor. Eagerly pouncing upon this, the detective quickly mastered its contents, which were simply as follows:--

"The second detachment will arrive at midnight to-night.--

"Zero."

Clearly it was not, therefore, a mere question of spying upon their position; but the evident intention of the cunning slaver was to send in small drafts of men to conceal themselves upon the mountain; and these, when his own army moved up to the attack, would, at a given signal, doubtless fall upon our friends in the rear, and thus effect a very serious diversion in favour of Zero, at a most critical moment.

The scheme was well thought-out, but the watchfulness of Kenyon had completely ruined it; and if the further suggestions which he now made should prove workable, the little band might be relied upon to read Master Zero another very severe and humiliating lesson, when he made his intended final onset.

Briefly, Kenyon's idea consisted of an attempt to lure the second detachment of slavers on to their utter destruction, but in view of their prematurely taking the alarm in consequence of our friends possibly failing to understand and correctly to answer their secret signals, a large party was to be slipped into the long grass of the veldt to intercept the slavers in the event of their making a push to escape, and an endeavour was to be made to capture some of the men alive, and force them to give up the secrets of their curious system of aerial correspondence.

Finally it was decided that Amaxosa should set out with ten of his own men and fifty of the warriors of the Atagbondo at moonrise, and lie in ambush about three miles to the north of the mountain, but this party was on no account to make any movement, except in the event of a rocket being fired from the camp, giving them the direction of the escaping slavers. The Zulu was especially cautioned against making fire signals of any kind, as it was calculated that the enemy would, themselves, probably employ these.

Little, however, did our friends know, as yet, of the devilish ingenuity of Master Zero, who had but to suspect the very remotest possibility of the existence of a trap to guard against it in most effectual fashion, and that night our friends received a peculiarly unpleasant proof of his dangerous capabilities in this direction.

The matter fell out thus:--As Kenyon, Leigh, and a party of fifty picked men were lying noiselessly in wait in the cover from which they had that morning driven the enemy, they were suddenly and viciously attacked, without a moment's warning, by Zero's forerunner, in the shape of an enormous jaguar, which severely mauled a number of the men ere he was settled by Kenyon, who drove a Zulu assegai through the beast's spine, whereupon his roarings woke every living echo in the country side, and a moment later a moving mass of dark forms could be seen gliding out from the friendly shadows cast by the mountain, and stringing themselves across the veldt in a vain effort to escape from their active foes.

Quickly Grenville sent up his rocket, and as the glittering thread of fire traced its way across the heavens, Leigh and his eager party dashed down the mountain, and followed the flying foe at speed across the veldt, fearing from their apparent strength that the slavers might prove too heavy for Amaxosa and his little band.

A mile from the rocks, finding their retreat cut off, the slavers formed in square and stood at bay between two fires. Leigh called to them to surrender, and lay down their arms, but the answer was hurled back in the shape of a contemptuous curse and a rattling volley, which stretched several of the Atagbondo upon the ground.

Not one moment after this could Leigh or Amaxosa restrain their men, who simply flung themselves upon the very muzzles of the slavers. Nothing short of a triple line of bayonets could have withstood such a magnificently audacious charge, and in less time than it takes to tell, the "People of the Stick" had literally wiped their hated foes off the face of the earth.

Five minutes covered the whole ghastly affair from beginning to end, and in that short space of time, Zero, in addition to the loss of his pet tiger, had suffered to the extent of fifty-three men, whilst our friends had on their side eleven killed outright and seventeen wounded, two of these last, dying the next day.

"Haow Inkoos," said the Zulu chief approvingly; "it is indeed a brave people, and fights well, almost as well as the Amazulu, but I would they used the assegai or the axe and made cleaner work of it. Well, what is done is done, my father, and these evil witch-finders will never trouble us again," and the great Zulu philosophically took a mighty pinch of snuff and offered one to Leigh in token of his entire satisfaction with the result of the night's work.

As soon as the arms had been collected, and the wounded men properly attended to, a council of war was held by the entire party, and under the circumstances it was considered useless to try and impose deceptive messages upon Zero, the more so as Kenyon himself was strongly of opinion, that not the pigeons, but the jaguar, had in the present instance been intended to carry back to Equatoria, news of the safe arrival of the band. The great cat would, of course, have been started off in the dark, without loss of time, or risk of suspicion even in the event of its being observed, and would certainly have travelled very swiftly to its distant home.

On the following morning the Atagbondo buried their dead, and then threw the deceased slavers into the river to carry a message of woe and weeping to their friends a hundred miles below.

Noticing his cousin looking anxiously at the summit of the mountain several times that day with Kenyon's field-glass, "What's the matter with the peak, old chap?" said Leigh.

"I wish I knew, Alf," was the reply; "I haven't seen it since the night we got here: ever since then it has been completely hidden by yonder white cloud, which rests upon it, and unless I am mistaken, the heat emanating from that vapour is so intense, that the everlasting snows are being absolutely melted away from the summit of the cone."

Just then a very wonderful and awful thing happened, for even as Grenville was speaking, the heat-clouds suddenly rolled away like a scroll and curled up out of sight, revealing the glittering peak for one brief instant in all the radiant majesty of its unveiled glory, and then the very next second there shot far, far up into the azure vault, a giant jet of angry, inky-looking smoke, which floated lightly and lazily through the absolutely pulseless air towards the north, and was quickly succeeded by another great puff, and another, until the whole of the northern heavens were densely clouded, and the mountain itself bore the appearance of a gigantic monster mechanically expelling vast volumes of dead black smoke at every labouring respiration of its mighty rock-girt lungs, and shrouding the whole country in a sombre death-like pall of weird and awful shade.

"A volcano, by Jove!" ejaculated Leigh.

"Yes," replied his cousin, "and an active one, too. I fear that Umbulanzi's explosion, the first night we came, has awakened the slumbering internal fires, or else the water is somehow penetrating into the crater and interfering with the gases imprisoned in its abysmal depths. We shall be in a nice pickle if the volcano takes a fancy to indulge in an eruption just at present; however, we must hope for the best, old man, and put our trust in Providence."

That very night, sad to say, our friends were awakened by the objectionable throes of a mighty earthquake; the rocks quaked and groaned, and the very bowels of the mountain were rent and torn by ear-splitting explosions, and in less than ten minutes the whole party was in full flight across the northern veldt, positively chased from the stronghold upon which they had bestowed so much labour by great streams of burning lava which, like vast rivers, flowed unimpeded down the mountain side, and, instantly setting the long grass on fire, caused our friends a most anxious time until they had safely crossed the river and got well away from the spot--their movements being rendered relatively slow by the necessity of carefully transporting the wounded men in hammocks.

After a short consultation it was decided to steer for the Hermit's Cave again, and to try and discover a place capable of defence somewhere in the immediate vicinity of Equatoria; for, with the exception of the mountain from which they had just been so rudely expelled, our friends were assured by the natives that no natural fastness of any kind existed within a hundred miles to the south of their present location, and southwards all, both black and white, absolutely declined to move until Zero was stamped out, or until they themselves were effectually disposed of in attempting to settle with him.

A very sharp look-out would have to be kept in order to avoid falling into the hands of the slavers, who were sure to notice the eruption of the volcano, and, knowing that the little band would have in consequence to relinquish the shelter afforded by the mountain, would doubtless be outlying with a view to falling upon them unawares; but by confining the travels of the party strictly to the night-time, and lying carefully hid by day, Grenville and Amaxosa hoped to bring all safely into the desired haven.

At all events, our friends were no worse off, in consequence of their journey to the peak, having, on the contrary, inflicted two crushing blows upon the enemy, and exchanged the bare handful of men with which they left Equatoria for a small army thoroughly equipped for war, already well-tried, and thirsting for occupation in the fighting line.

Chapter 13: In Freedom's Cause

Owing to the difficulty of transporting so many wounded men, it took our friends quite four days to accomplish the distance which they had covered on a former occasion in less than one-half that time; but by the fourth night all had safely reached the mountains of the north, and after Amaxosa had carefully reconnoitred the vicinity of the hermit's cave, the party took undisputed possession thereof, and made arrangements to defend the place in the event of an attack, by throwing up a great earthwork round the outlet of the cavern.

This important matter attended to, Grenville and Kenyon next proceeded to explore, by torchlight, the labyrinth of caves with which the heart of the mountain proved to be honeycombed, and in the furthest of those natural vaulted chambers they finally discovered Muzi Zimba the Ancient. The old man was in a state of very great prostration, and was obviously dying from sheer decay of all his faculties. Kenyon at once administered to him a spoonful of brandy, and afterwards prevailed upon him to swallow some beef-tea. This grateful nourishment soon appeared to revive his sinking form, and, recognising Grenville, he accorded him a hearty welcome, and congratulated him kindly upon his marvellous escape from death, and then, speaking very lucidly, his mental faculties seeming to grow clearer as his bodily vigour gradually died out, he dilated at some length to the attentive pair, upon their present dangerous position, and regarding the cause and the remedy for the horrors of the slave-trade.

It must not, however, be supposed that the conversation given here, is written down precisely as it was spoken; for at times our friends had much ado to keep the poor old man alive, and it was only by continually giving him weak stimulants, that body and soul were kept together until his work was done. Often, too, his halting tongue refused to frame the meanings he desired to convey, and Grenville had thus frequently to come to his assistance, and express his thoughts for him in clear, every-day English.

"My sons," said the aged man, "I came hither many, many years ago--how many, I know not, for my mind has for a long and weary time been under a very darksome cloud, but it is clearer now, and in the light which streams through heaven's wide-open gates. I once more see, with the eye of faith, and know that

76

all will yet again be well. Hearken, my sons, for I can tell ye much that may avail ye to escape from the hands of the demon who dwells in yonder city of evil.

"Ye are brave men, and I have heard how that ye have already rescued many precious lives from this fiend in human form, and have thrice brought defeat and disaster upon his hateful arms. Nevertheless, be ye ware, my sons, for he has, indeed, a very great army of bloody-minded and wicked men, and he has, moreover, sworn to entirely eat you up. Know, therefore, that in the third cave from here is a spot where, by moving a great black stone, a narrow passage can be found, but wide enough for two men to walk abreast, and this leads gently downwards, step by step, right through the bowels of the mountain, and so into the town of the evil ones, where there are many white and black slaves, both of men and women. Mark this passage well, my children, for if once yon monster wins the secret of the way, ye, too, will exist only as I do-- even midway between the bitter memories of the unforgotten past and the golden shores of the great hereafter.

"And now, my sons, bear with me yet, regarding this shameful trade in human flesh and blood. Long years ere Zero came hither, like a curse, this country was peaceful and all happy, and much did I teach the simple people that tended to the welfare of both soul and body; but since the coming of this man of sin, all has been turned again to evil, and the land everywhere weeps tears of sorrow and of blood.

"What can we do more, my sons, we who, simply placing our lives in the hands of the good God who gave them, penetrate unarmed, and with naught of defence but the Gospel of Peace, to the furthest confines of this dark land? What, I say, can we do, when the misguided rulers of Christian countries at home daily permit--nay, encourage--the unrestricted sale to the wretched natives, of millions of gallons of a very evil drink, which goes by the name of 'square face,' but which the traders declare to be but harmless gin. Gin! my sons, the first coat of which is under one shilling a gallon, and which is poured into the land, after it has paid the British governors upon the western sea-girt border of this mighty continent a duty of half-a-crown a gallon, or equal to two-and-a-half times its cost. Look what follows. The already debased African is at once reduced below the level of the very beasts that perish. He must have this fiery spirit, the first fatal draught of which has inflamed his soul, and brought into active being every vicious slumbering detail of his fallen human nature, and in order to obtain the wherewithal to purchase the beloved 'Square Face,' he falls unawares upon his next-door neighbour, so to speak--perhaps upon his own familiar friend, who trusts him--and carrying him off by night, secretly sells him to the highest bidder, white or black, that he can find within easy distance of his home.

"The trade in gin and rum is at the bottom of one-half of this evil slave-dealing, and so long as this crying sin is not only permitted, but encouraged, amongst a simple people, who have no more judgment to exercise, than have a third of the weak-minded ones sheltered from the cruel world in many a private mad-house, so long will Central Africa remain a country where cruelty and misery, and the shedding of blood, prevail, where men bow down to stocks and stones, where Satan's kingdom is, and where the missionary, my sons, is little more than a useless martyr, his precious life expended in the lively faith that the mighty power of his God will cause the barren soil he waters with his blood to prove a fruitful field before the great day of reckoning comes for missionary, for slaver, and for the miserable aboriginal African, whose body and soul these opposing forces contend for mightily both night and day.

"Hear me further, my sons, for much good may yet be done, in spite of Zero and of the Arabs, who accomplish a world of evil, if someone of the great white nations of the world will but come forward and use its God-given strength for the purpose of putting down the slave-trade, suppressing entirely the sale of gin and rum in Africa, and supporting the missionaries. Africa! The whole country is being depopulated, and every acre of it watered with the tears of a people torn from their happy homes and sold into slavery in distant lands, or sent across the seas, and soon this vast and fertile region, as yet almost unknown to the white races, will become in all directions an impenetrable and useless jungle, through which even the mammoth elephant must fail to force his way--a dark continent in very deed and truth, an eyesore to both God and man.

"In the earlier days of my sojourn in this place, my sons, I looked to free and happy England to do all that this rich and fruitful land required to make it perfect; and I taught the natives, under God, to reverence and to pray for the Great White Queen, their mother, in whose all-powerful name I came to them in Freedom's cause. Alas! my sons, the first slaver who entered here and broke up their quiet homes was this shameless scoundrel Zero; and, speaking with the same tongue as my own, naught of difference could this people see between his land and mine; and then worse, far worse, when the horrible slave traffic attracted hither the native dealers from the farther west, these brought with them word that slaves could be freely sold under French and German, and--oh! the shame of it--under

British rule, ay, under Freedom's own flag on the utmost coast of Western Equatorial Africa.

"My sons, I credited it not, and I sent my trusted runner a journey of many, many weary moons, and he brought me back a faithful word--alas! that it should have been a true one.

"The thing is even so, my father,' he said. Almost within the very cities of the Great White Queen, where the moving water beats, ever murmuring, upon the yellow sands, and within hearing of the guns of British forts, I saw very many slaves; and these were sold from house to house, or from land to land, as their owners in the towns desired. Also, day by day I watched great caravans of slaves from the peoples of many, many powerful kingdoms, bringing in native produce and dust of gold, and carrying out very many cases of square face and of rum.'

"It is a false report that ye bring,' I said; how know ye that the men were slaves? The Great White Queen frees all who come beneath the shadow of her glorious flag.'

"That may be,' he said, as I saw not the Great White Queen herself, but the slaves were there, all marked with a brand on the cheek, my father. Also, I had speech of some of these, and they said that they were slaves. More, my father, there are also in the cities many native guards, and most of these men are also slaves, who serve under the Queen's ruler for money, which they give to the owners of their bodies whenever the Queen pays them; and so, my father, I would even live here under your shadow, where I and my people are free by the strength of our own right hands, than be a pining slave under the flag of the Great White Queen, my mother, who is too far away to help her suffering children when they cry out of wrong and find none to hear them.'

"Then it was, my sons," said the aged man, "that I lost my reason; I could not eat my food, and my sleep at nights went from me; I could only kneel and humbly pray, both night and day, to the good God on high that lie would wake the ear of our gracious Queen to hear the pitiful cry of these poor defenceless creatures, over whom he has given her an empire, and power, and glory, and who, though they are so far from her, are yet her loyal subjects, and very near to the great God Himself, in whose hand her breath is, and whose are all her ways.

"And now, my sons, my eyes are closing fast, and I leave ye to follow me along the weary road which leads to the great hereafter. Take, then, the last blessing of a very aged and a defenceless man, to whom ye were both kind and good. Fear God, and follow that which is good, so shall we meet again in the land where sorrows are forgotten, and where peace and rest await both you and me. Greeting, then, my sons, to you and yours--greeting and farewell!"

And so he died, this one staunch witness for freedom and his God, in a land where all else was foul and evil. Very peacefully his life slipped from him with the dawn of day, and his loyal spirit soared to the very presence of Him who gave it life.

"God rest him," said Grenville gently; "God rest His faithful servant. May I too die the death of a brave man, and may my last end be even as the end of Muzi Zimba the Ancient."

That same day the little band buried the hermit's body, the natives following him to the grave with many marks of respect and reverence, and the white men firing a farewell salute over the last resting-place of this gallant soldier, who had given up his life for the truth, and died in freedom's cause, in this far-distant land.

Chapter 14: Equatoria

As soon as our friends had paid the final honours to the mortal remains of Muzi Zimba, they carefully warned the "People of the Stick" against spreading the news of his decease in any shape or form, fearing that the ignorant natives in the surrounding country might foolishly impute his somewhat sudden and unexpected end, to the unauthorised presence of the little hand in his cavernous dwelling.

Hardly were the funeral obsequies over than Kenyon drew Grenville aside, and after a few moments of earnest conversation, the pair announced their intention of investigating the secret stair through the mountain, of which the old hermit had spoken to them.

Taking Amaxosa along, and supplying themselves from Muzi Zimba's ample stores with torches made of fibre, the trio entered the indicated cave, shifted the black, basaltic-looking rock, and duly found themselves in the entrance of the tunnel. The tortuous way was rough and very narrow, but it was, as the old man had said, fairly easy to traverse, and in twenty minutes' time our friends emerged into semi-daylight in the narrow shaft of a dry and disused well, from whence-- by means of a stout but roughly-constructed ladder of rope, which hung from its upper orifice--the old man had evidently obtained access at will into the slavers' town.

Withdrawing cautiously into the mountain again, in fear lest the smoke of their torches should be seen above the mouth of the well, our friends entered into a somewhat heated argument.

Grenville was for entirely closing the narrow passage by blocking it once for all with mighty rocks, which would effectually prevent Zero from discovering the secret of the way, and perhaps destroying themselves and their cavern by an explosion of gunpowder; but Kenyon declared that, sooner than permit such a capital means of access to Equatoria to be destroyed, he would himself sit and watch it night and day. His specious arguments and professional instinct, at length prevailed over Grenville's caution, and the trio then resolved that two reliable men should be kept constantly on the watch beneath the well, provided with a cord, the other end of which they would attach to the trigger of a small

81

pistol fixed in the cavern above, and should anyone attempt to descend the well, the sentinels were to jerk the cord, fire the pistol as an anxious call for help, and forthwith retreat noiselessly into the mountain burrow, where they would be met at the narrowest part of the tortuous path by armed support.

During the whole of that day the party on the rock could descry in the far distance large bands of the slaver fraternity patrolling the southern veldt, and carefully searching the borders of the eastern forest, being evidently altogether at a loss to know what had become of the dangerous and hated foe, and yearning, no doubt, for the resuscitation of their slaughtered bloodhounds; whilst when night fell, the furthest limit of vision revealed, a hundred miles away, the fire-girt summit of the fierce volcano, its blazing peak hanging upon the distant line of smoke-beclouded sky like a glittering star of the first magnitude.

The night was very dark and moonless when Kenyon and Amaxosa left the outer cave to relieve Leigh and Grenville, who were keeping watch below the well; but, pausing before he entered the narrow passage, the American sent the Zulu forward, simply saying he would join him by-and-by, as he had yet some work to do, and so it came to pass that the two cousins returned to the cavern without having seen him, and that Amaxosa, keeping his lonely vigil by torchlight, passed through the most fearsome trial his courageous but untutored heart had ever known; for whilst he watched and waited, patient as a statue carved in stone, the great Zulu heard a light footfall behind him, and, turning quickly, beheld, to his utter horror, the well-known figure of the ancient Muzi Zimba approaching through the gloom. The warrior's heart stood still with fear and his very blood froze in his veins--Muzi Zimba, whose dead body he had that very day helped to consign to its grave, and upon whose breast he had placed giant rocks to scare the beasts of prey; yet here he stood, and there before him in the flesh stood Muzi Zimba. Nay, it could not be flesh and blood, but a spook (spirit) of the mountain, and not even a child of the Undi could fight with spooks. Coming swiftly to him, the vision spoke quietly to him in broken Zulu. "Greeting," it said, "greeting, Lion of the Undi, what dost thou here by night in Muzi Zimba's secret way."

"Greeting, great Father of the Spooks," boldly answered the Zulu. "I do this here, I watch thy dark and narrow stair, oh, Ancient One, by order of the Great White Chief, my father, and if any enter to disturb thy restful peace, he dies a swift and easy death on this my ready spear."

"Well done, Amaxosa," was the cool reply which the astonished chief received from his ancient friend, the "Father of the Spooks," as the dread thing deftly removed its flowing wealth of beard and whiskers, and revealed the clean-shaved countenance of Stanforth Kenyon, the American detective.

"Wow, Inkoos!" said the astonished Zulu. "Wow! The thing was indeed well done; and I, even I, the son of the witch-doctor, Isanusi, would have let thee pass and leave me for a spook. Yet, did it seem strange to me, my father, thou shouldst speak to thy son with the tongue of his own people, forever I heard that the Ancient One who has gone from us, knew not to speak as speak the children of the Zulu."

Briefly explaining his intentions to the chief, Kenyon carefully readjusted his disguise, and, nimbly mounting the ladder of rope, scrambled out of the mouth of the well, and at once found himself in a clump of bushes, and close to the outskirts of the slavers' town, towards which he fearlessly directed his now seemingly feeble steps.

Well was it for Stanforth Kenyon that years of rigid training in his own peculiar walk of life enabled him to support to perfection the somewhat difficult, because exquisitely simple, character, which his supreme audacity had undertaken. The extreme darkness of the night was, however, favourable to his enterprise, as there were but few people about, and the detective found himself in the very centre of Equatoria without being accosted by anyone. The town, to his surprise, proved to be very compactly built, and consisted of perhaps five hundred houses, mostly composed of wood and roofed with iron, the only exceptions to this rule being what were evidently the public offices of the place, which were built of a mixture of sand and gravel, a composition going amongst the natives by the name of "swish," and which presented, so far as he could see by the light of the oil-lamps hung round the buildings, an extremely handsome appearance.

Just as Kenyon was about to move forward after carefully taking stock of the place, a young girl started out from a side street, and laid a gently detaining hand upon his arm.

"Father," she said, "I have looked and longed for thee every night, and feared that thou wert ill. Come and see my boy, I beseech thee, good father, for he dies--he dies before my face, and here is none to help but thee."

With a sign of brief assent, the detective turned and halted slowly along, despite the manifest impatience of the young and anxious mother.

Turning into a small house some little way along the street, she led him

83

through a comfortably but roughly furnished parlour, into a bed-room at the rear, where lay a baby boy not more than eighteen months old, and whom his medical experience soon assured him was suffering from a slight attack of that most malignant disease, diphtheria.

Knowing, through Grenville, that the old hermit had acted in the capacity of physician and surgeon to both slavers and natives, Kenyon, before he left the cavern, had provided himself with several articles, including a small case of phials, likely to be of use in supporting his assumption of the character of a medical practitioner; and, briefly directing the young mother to keep the child quiet and supply him with cooling drinks, he carefully painted the tonsils with perchloride of iron, and left her instructions to continue this treatment.

As Kenyon, however, was moving away, the grateful mother again stopped him. "Father," she said, "I call thee such by permission; canst thou do naught for yon poor woman whom these cruel, heartless Mormons have condemned to death by fire, because she will not change her faith and `marry' one of their own creatures. Thou knowest my history, my father; how I was stolen away when but a girl, and wedded to a man I used to hate, and that my happiest hour was when he died in battle. Yet do I love my little son, and could I but give freedom to this woman I would fly the country with her, and take refuge with the brave men of my own race who have escaped hence, and who now hold Zero at defiance."

"Where lies this woman, my daughter?" said the false hermit, after making a show of thinking carefully for some little time.

"Still in the same strong place, my father--the great hall of the common prison-house; and at noon, next day but one, she suffers at the stake. Save her, if thou canst, my father; and if it be indeed beyond thy power, then give her, in mercy, a draught of swift and deadly poison, if thou hast such, and earn a double blessing from her ere she dies."

With a promise that he would endeavour on the following night to see the condemned one referred to, our adventurer at length got away from the importunate woman, and effected, undiscovered, his retreat to the well, and thence into the depths of the mountain, where he, of course, found the Zulu on guard, the pair being soon after this relieved by Umbulanzi and the young Scotsman, Ewan, of whom all had formed a high opinion, both as to shrewdness and bravery.

Arrived in the cave above, Kenyon communicated to his astonished and admiring friends his experiment and the result of it, and all then fell to eagerly discussing ways and means for the rescue of the poor condemned woman from her villainous judges and would-be executioners; and, ere the party lay down to sleep, it was decided that Kenyon should make an attempt to see her the following night in his character of a priest, and learn what suggestions the captive could herself make, with regard to a plan to save her life and give her back her liberty.

Chapter 15: Hope

On the following night, therefore, as soon as darkness fell, Kenyon, disguised to represent the old hermit, again entered the slavers' town, whilst Leigh, Grenville, Amaxosa, and a score of picked men lay in wait below the well, from which, in the event of hearing a given signal whistle, they were to sally out and assist our adventurous friend.

The detective went about his accustomed work with the greatest nonchalance; and, on reaching the building which had been pointed out to him the previous night, simply and plainly told the guard that he wished to have speech of the condemned woman. Without a word of reply, one of the men on duty signed to Kenyon to follow him, and well might our adventurer, under the loose folds of his cloak, clench his fingers over the butt of a friendly revolver when he found himself ushered directly into the well-known and hated presence of Zero the Slaver. For a moment the impulse was almost unconquerable in Kenyon to slip out his six-shooter and make an end of this inhuman monster without further palaver; but, recognising how much hung upon the result of his actions that night, he wisely restrained his passions.

The slaver was sitting in a handsomely got-up room carpeted with furs, and thick with weapons and with trophies of the chase, and opposite to him--fortunately, perhaps, for Kenyon--sat the native king already spoken of, and who immediately did our adventurer reverence, in his capacity of Muzi Zimba the Ancient.

As the guard detailed his errand. Zero rose with a sneering laugh. "Ay! let him go to her," he said, "and look 'ee here, old man, if this captive escapes me as did the last ones, thine own life shall pay the forfeit. Now go, nay, by all the Gods, I will go too!" and, passing on in front of the supposed hermit, he provided Kenyon with another almost overpowering temptation to use his weapons.

Unbarring the door of another room, Zero let the hermit in and closed the portal behind them both, and Kenyon found himself face to face with an imperially beautiful woman, still quite young, but whose lovely face was worn with sorrow and anguish, and furrowed with her bitter tears. A tall, well-knit figure, a wealth of lustrous golden hair, and glorious deep blue eyes, formed a tout ensemble which might have won pity from a stone, but had no effect whatever upon this scoundrel who battened on human misery.

"Well, madam," said the slaver, in cutting tones, "you have your own obstinacy to thank for your death, which takes place to-morrow. Here's a priest for you, so be quick and say your patter, or whatever it is. You'd be surprised to see how fast your precious boy is picking up the tenets of our Holy Mormon Faith," and the demon laughed a jeering, taunting laugh, which made Kenyon's blood boil, and he could have kissed the feet of the defenceless woman before him for the gesture of ineffable contempt with which she turned her back on the wretched hound. "Pray, begone," she said in a firm but musical voice; "your hated presence comes between me and my God."

"Ha! ha!" laughed the sardonic ruffian; "one for you, Sir Priest, one for you, I reckon. Well, come along with you, I've no time to fool away here." But Kenyon, mindful of the part he had to play, took not the slightest notice of the slaver, but kneeled reverently down by himself for a few brief moments, then rose and left the room obedient to an impatient signal from the fierce and wicked man, whom his fingers fairly itched to throttle then and there.

Had Zero looked behind him he would have been greatly astonished to see the captive woman bend simply down and gaze wildly at the floor beneath her feet; and then, in a mighty revulsion of feeling, give way to a perfect paroxysm of tears and sobs. What, you ask, gentle reader, was the cause of this sudden and subtle change from strength to weakness? What? Simply Stanforth Kenyon's message written with the point of his finger on a dusty boarded floor, and that message was:

"Hope."

Only four precious letters; yet this man had written them at the peril of his life. It must, it did, mean something, and all her woman's wit was instantly on the alert to lay hold of the earliest clue to the whereabouts of these her secret friends.

Hope! Oh pity her, gentle reader, a lovely woman in the zenith of her beauty and the pride of motherhood, condemned to die a frightful death before another day had run its course, and die merely to satisfy the insensate malice of a ruffian Mormon hound.

Turning away from Zero, Kenyon would have left the building in silence; but the slaver laid upon his shoulder a firm, detaining hand. "Softly, my good old man! `Softly! softly! catch monkey,' as these infernal niggers say. You live on the mountain, and I reckon you can see a long way. Now have you seen naught of this cursed Grenville and the pack of fools who follow him? Speak out, man, or I guess I'll soon find means to open your wretched old jaws."

Like a flash of light, an inspiration came to Kenyon; and, drawing himself up proudly, he shook off the slaver's hand. "The men ye name are even now within my cave upon the hill," he said. "Go seek them if ye dare, monster of evil, but beware the end thereof; beware, for Muzi Zimba warns thee!"

The effect was precisely what Kenyon had calculated upon. Flinging the old man from him with a fearful oath, the slaver sent his powerful voice echoing through the house and out along the streets, calling up guards and officers in every direction, whilst our adventurous friend soon after took his departure, entirely unnoticed during the tumult which followed the communication of the news which he had given, regarding the position of his friends.

Hanging about for a few moments, however, Kenyon learned all he wished to know, as he heard Zero, with a volley of oaths, exclaim: "Put off her execution? No, by all the Gods--no, tie the slut to the faggots at noon to-morrow, and let her roast, and mind you have her whelp of a son to watch her die, whilst I eat up these cursed fools who think to change my vengeance and to spoil my trade."

This was all that Kenyon required to know, and an hour later he was deep in consultation with his friends in the hermit's cave, amongst the northern hills.

It was agreed on all hands that Kenyon had acted for the best, as the plan he had formed, though simple in the extreme, had every promise of a grand success.

Briefly, the scheme stood thus:--Whilst Zero was moving up to the attack, as he evidently meant to do next morning, a party of their own was, by way of the secret passage and the well, to enter Equatoria, fall upon the few guards left there, carry off the captive woman, and generally do as much damage to the slavers' town as they found it in their power to accomplish. It was calculated that the rifles of Leigh, Umbulanzi, and Ewan, supported by the Atagbondo marksmen, would be quite sufficient to check Zero in his ascent up the steep and difficult path to the cavern; and, even if he forced his way so far, he would have to reckon with about two hundred of the Atagbondo, and would find their warriors uncommonly hard nuts to crack; whilst Kenyon and Grenville, who were to assail the town, would take with them Amaxosa and his men, together with a hundred of the "People of the Stick," quite sufficient, they thought, to do irreparable damage to the slavers' home in the two hours which they promised themselves to spend in Equatoria.

And so, after looking carefully over their arms and their defences, the little band lay down to sleep that night with perfect confidence in their leaders, and in the issues of the morrow; only Leigh sat up the whole night cleaning his weapons, with murder in his heart, and a wealth of determined resolve upon his handsome face.

Chapter 16: Alive from the Dead

Soon after dawn the whole party was astir, and the defenders of the cave were quickly at their several posts, whilst Kenyon and Grenville again carefully looked over their plan of attack.

Grenville was fortunately able to define the probable site of the execution, knowing from experience, that the miserable victims done to death by the infamous Mormon Inquisitors were either burned alive or crucified upon a small natural hill--a curious smooth-topped, skull-shaped mound, in fact, perhaps fifty feet in height, and which, fortunately, stood between the mouth of the old well and the slavers' town, and was equi-distant from each, perhaps five or six yards. It was a shrewd count, therefore, that the little rescue-party would be able to get within easy rifle range before they were discovered by the enemy; and, as Zero would be certain to carry practically the whole of the fighting population with him, it was extremely probable that when our friends unmasked their party, a general stampede for safety on the part of the slavers would be the immediate result, when it was hoped that the poor captive woman would be quite forgotten, and, being left behind, would prove an easy acquisition, and when they once had her in safety, the hands of our friends would, of course, be perfectly free to act in the way that might seem best.

At eleven o'clock the leaders of the storming party exchanged a warm hand-grasp with Leigh and Umbulanzi, and left the cavern by way of the tunnel, through which we will now follow their fortunes.

The getting of such a relatively large number of men down through this singular mountain burrow and up beyond the mouth of the well on the other side of the range, took considerably longer than the detective had reckoned upon, and the hour was within a very few minutes of noon by the time that all were safely hidden in the straggling line of bush which masked their presence, and impinged upon the narrow stretch of veldt lying between their position and the curious knoll referred to, upon which, to their horror, our friends could now plainly see a great upright stake fixed, and around this post were placed bundles of heavy faggots, packed closely with a resinous, woody fibre, and even while they looked, the executioner appeared upon the hill, carrying in his hand a swinging

90

brazier, filled with some burning substance.

Grenville quickly pointed out that the victim was to be faced towards the town, which was another circumstance in their favour, as the crest of the knoll would effectually screen their movements from the preoccupied herd of sightseers beyond.

All hearts beat fast as they saw the poor sufferer led up and bound to the martyr stake, whilst the mighty, spontaneous shout which went up to heaven, caused each man's fingers to clinch anxiously upon his weapons, as it proved to them that the multitude beyond the knoll could be no inconsiderable one.

The instant that the executioner turned his back upon the well, and busied himself with the fastening of the poor woman to the stake, Grenville gave the word, and the whole party as one man shot noiselessly out of the bush, and commenced a jog-trot across the open space which separated them from the scene of the execution. When all were within a hundred yards, the wretched fellow upon the hill turned him round and saw them; then uttering a wild shout, and hurriedly bending down, he seized a lighted brand and endeavoured, with trembling hands, to thrust it in amongst the faggots.

Dropping quickly upon one knee, Grenville raised his rifle, but still somewhat weak and shaken by the sharp run, for once he missed his man. Kenyon, however, quickly following, "wiped his eye," knocking the rascal head-over-heels off the hill.

A great roar of surprise and wonder burst from the mob beyond the knoll, changed to a shriek of terror and consternation as the fierce Zulus sent their wild battle-cry echoing across the rolling veldt, and charged right up the hill, instantly surrounding the poor creature at the stoke, and killing the Mormon satellites who were clambering up to the spot.

And now ensued a stubborn fight, for Zero had left behind him many more men than our friends had counted upon, and these, having mostly left their rifles behind them in the town, charged madly up the little hill, and furiously engaged the rescue-party hand-to-hand, and for quite five minutes the cause of all this tumult was utterly forgotten, whilst the fight swung fiercely to and fro, and the issue hung in doubt. Our friends certainly had the advantage of position, whilst the slavers, on the other hand, still stood in the proportion of at least two to one; but the fiery valour of the active Zulus, nobly backed by the almost insensate fury of the injured "People of the Stick," would brook no living check, and presently, led by Amaxosa, they went right through the slaver crowd, cutting them down on every hand, and driving all that were left of the wretched men pell-mell into the town, which both bands entered simultaneously.

Kenyon then bethought him of the prisoner, and, taking Grenville back, both men turned to ascend the hill, and relieve the poor girl from her painful and dangerous position. Still as a statue she stood, with her head drooping forward upon her breast, and for one moment the thought that some stray shot had struck her crossed painfully the minds of both; but when they had arrived within twenty yards of her position the girl heard them, and quickly raised her head, her beautiful face all wet with tears, and eloquent with voiceless prayers to heaven. Staggering back, as if struck by a shot, Grenville, to Kenyon's utter astonishment, dropped his gun, and threw up his hands in a frenzy of terror.

"God in heaven!" he screamed, "Dora, sister Dora! or am I mad, indeed."

Well might poor Grenville think his brain had turned. After all Zero's wicked boasts of crime, and all his cousin's bitter sorrow for his long-dead wife, how could he believe that there before him, in the flesh, beautiful as when first he saw her in East Utah, stood Dora, Lady Drelincourt, dressed in deep black, with a pure white cross upon her breast, and fastened to a martyr's stake, in the darkest part of darkest Equatorial Africa?

"Dick!" she cried, "dear Dick Grenville, tell me, does my darling husband live, or have I lost him, too. Tell me, tell me! I beseech you, for the love of God."

Pulling himself together, as the music of those well-known accents reached his ears, Grenville at once ran to the poor girl's side, and quickly unbound the chain which fixed her to the cruel stake, speaking meanwhile soothing words of hope and joy, and peace on earth, whilst Kenyon, hearing that her boy was in the town, went off, like an arrow from the bow, to make certain of the safety of his friend and patron's little son.

In every direction, as the detective entered the town, he found blazing houses, and dead and dying men, but the Atagbondo had behaved splendidly, and set a lesson to their evil white-skinned foes, in this respect, that on woman or on child they laid no hand, but every man they found died by the spear or by "the stick." One ghastly sight, however, did Kenyon see, for absolutely pinned to a burning house by a Zulu assegai, which had passed right through her heart, hung the dead mistress of Zero, the slaver-chief, and the beholder know that the hand that killed her was the hand of justice--justice on a woman more evil in her ways than many a wicked man who had that day fallen in fair fight.

Cornered, like rats, and yet more numerous than their fierce opponents, the slavers fought with all the Courage of despair, but naught availed them, and soon the only house in Equatoria which remained intact, was the great public hall, into which the storming party had collected the entire movable wealth of the slaver fraternity, and from the roof of which the Saint George's ensign now floated lazily upon the labouring breeze. Seeing the good old flag, Grenville at once led his rescued "sister," as it was always his habit to call her, back to the Mormon town, and the anxious young mother forgot the awful scenes of carnage and of blood, in the joy of embracing, once more, her loving little child.

Ordering the men to shoulder everything worth having, and to return to the upper cave before Zero and his band could arrive, Grenville and Kenyon prepared to leave Equatoria, accompanied by Lady Drelincourt and her son, and by the woman of whom mention has previously been made, together with her child, who was now in better health, whilst the whole of the Mormon-cum-slaver women and children had scampered away to the woods, which lay in the rear of the town.

Just now, however, the victorious little band received a very severe check, for ere they reached the skull-shaped hill, the report of firearms broke upon their ears, and Grenville suddenly exclaimed, "By Jove! What can have happened? There goes Alf's repeater. What, in the name of fortune, is he doing here?"

Dashing up the hill, and leaving the women in shelter on the town side of it, they came upon a sad sight. Right below their position, Leigh and about a hundred men only, were sullenly falling back upon the knoll, fighting every inch of the ground like fiends, but being steadily driven in, by something like seven times their number of heavily-armed slavers.

As the retreating party got against the hill, the slavers uttered a shout of triumph, and charging in, drove the little band in every direction; but little they reckoned upon the thunderbolt which fell upon them from above. Down from the top of the knoll like a living, irresistible whirlwind, came the lion-hearted children of the Zulu, led by their fierce and active chief, and close upon their heels, in a compact serried mass, followed the ready "People of the Stick," behind whom Leigh and his gallant little band re-formed and charged the slavers home.

By this time the rifles were almost silent, only Grenville's piece occasionally speaking its mind, for he seemed to have eyes for every combat of a friend, and when the great Zulu had led his men clean through the heart of the slavers, and had charged madly back again along a ghastly lane of dead and dying men, the foe drew off a little, and sought to load his guns.

This would never do, and with a wild earth-shaking shout, Amaxosa again charged the craven crowd; with him came the staunch war-dogs of the Zulu, who loved the slaughter as they loved their daring chief, and scarce a rod behind came Barad "the Hailstorm," his faithful people following into the very jaws of death the gallant "Chieftain of the Stick," and ever side by side with the mighty Zulu, there fought Alf Leigh, scarcely less fierce than his sable friend, and even more determined; and before the "giant three" the foe fell in every direction, like corn beneath the sickle.

Suddenly, however, Leigh broke out of the line, and, with a wild cry of triumph, fiercely engaged Zero himself, hand to hand, and axe to axe. The slaver-chief was a powerful and an active man, but he was no match for the colossal Englishman, to whom fury, revenge, and long-nursed bitter hate, had given a tenfold strength, and in ten seconds Zero lay wounded and stunned upon the ground.

Then there arose a mighty uproar, the slavers charged madly in upon the foe, and bore them back a dozen rods, fighting the while like fiends, and thus succeeded in carrying their wounded chieftain off the field, then surging in around the little band which was now fighting in square, the desperate slavers made a tremendous effort to annihilate their plucky and determined foes. Clubs are poor weapons to keep the face of a square, and the formation was quickly broken, and, fighting like lions, our friends were driven backward to the hill, every one of them fairly drenched with blood, and almost all wounded, whilst their number now totalled something under a hundred men.

All about lay the slain, singly and in knots and heaps; dead men everywhere, and everywhere rivers of blood, and the horrid stench of slaughter.

After a few moments' rest, the slavers charged in with a wild shout, resolved, at all cost, to wipe out the little band of heroes who held the skull-shaped hill; and when the surging struggling mass of men had been lost in a rain of blows, for full ten minutes, all chance of escape or triumph for our friends seemed gone: but fifty men were left to fight three hundred.

Grenville and Leigh, Amaxosa and Kenyon, were back to back, their blows rained straight and sure, and at every blow from each a man went down, still what could they do against such overwhelming odds as six to one.

Down went the gallant Umbulanzi, with a great spear wound in his back, and down upon his breathless corpse went his recreant foe, his head split to the very

94

chin by a vengeful blow from Grenville's ready axe.

All was in vain, yet even as our friends had given up all hope of escaping from the hideous crowd which surged in upon them like hungry wolves round a dying buffalo, a clear, cold voice rang out in stentorian tones across the startled veldt, arresting every hand and every arm.

"Cease," it said; "cease and hold your hands, ye uncircumcised ones, both white and black, unless ye wish to die." And there upon the knoll, to the utter horror of our friends, flaunted the dreaded banner of Mormonism, and round the mingled mass of combatants, and of dead and dying men, there extended on every hand a mighty triple ring of armed and hated followers of the False Prophet.

Ringed in by fully a thousand well-armed men, further resistance was worse than useless. Moreover, Grenville's keen eye quickly noted the curious fact that, so far from displaying anything like enthusiasm over the advent of the Mormon host, the slavers seemed considerably more taken aback by the presence of the new arrivals than even his own party.

The tension of feeling between the three bands was all at once unintentionally relieved by poor Leigh suddenly noticing Dora on the crest of the knoll, where the poor girl had been an agonised spectator of the awful fight, and where her cries, notifying the dreaded Mormon approach, had been no more audible than the twitterings of a sparrow. Suddenly noticing her, I say, an expression of positive terror froze poor Leigh's face, his hair rose up upon his head, and with a fearful shriek of "Dora, Dora, my long-dead, darling wife!" he threw up his hands and fell prone upon his face, with the life-blood welling from his mouth.

Kenyon threw himself upon his knees beside his friend, but in another instant Dora was holding her lover's head upon her lap, lover and husband both in one, lost and found; and, after all these cruel years of weary waiting, must she find her darling but to lose his love for ever? No! for the good God was full of mercy to the faithful heart that had trusted Him to the very stake of martyrdom, and her husband soon came round again, but to relapse into a dangerous attack of brain fever, from which he escaped only by slow degrees, and it took many weary months and a world of anxious nursing night and day ere Alfred Leigh regained his normal strength.

Speaking again, the Mormon leader, a fine-looking old man, with a snow-white beard, commanded the combatants to lay down their arms and consider themselves the prisoners of the Holy Three, and this order the slavers instantly obeyed.

Stepping coolly forward, however, Grenville spoke up boldly--

"Who are you, and by what right do you command here, sir? Yonder floats the flag of England, under which we serve, and we demand that you respect its world-wide rights."

"Richard Grenville, I know you," was the cool reply, "and here I command everyone by the right of might, so lay down your arms, or my men shall sweep you off the face of the earth and save further trouble: ay, both you and yonder heap of carrion with you," and the Mormon pointed to the slavers, who were huddled together a hundred yards distant from their late antagonists.

Clearly the game was up, and there was nothing for it but to comply with the Mormon's commands, which all did with a very ill grace, when, commencing with the slavers, they were quickly bound; but, coming swiftly to Grenville the Mormon leader spoke.

"I know," he said, "that ye are brave and upright, but bloody-minded men, yet is your word your bond, and if ye give it me now that ye will not essay escape, no cord or chain shall touch ye or this your giant friend," and he pointed to the great Zulu, who was painted a ghastly red from head to foot.

Eagerly thanking the Mormon, all gladly gave the required parole, and, under this man's direction, they then carried Leigh into a room in the public offices and left him there with his wife and child; after which, by permission, Kenyon first attended to the wounds of his own party, and afterwards to those of the slavers, though the old Mormon cynically remarked to him that it would be much more merciful to let the scoundrels die at once.

A curious meeting it was in Central Africa between the detective and his quarry, when this amateur doctor came to the point of exercising his healing art upon the fallen Zero.

"Well, Monckton Bassett, we meet again," said Kenyon, coolly; "and now let me look at this head of yours, for I should be sorry for you to go off the ropes without Uncle Sam having a hand in the affair."

For reply Zero hurled a fearful curse at the detective, and ordered him to begone, so Kenyon calmly left the scoundrel to himself.

Chapter 17: Quod Dixi Dixi

As soon as opportunity offered, Grenville closely questioned the Chieftain of the Stick as to the manner in which his party, commanded by Leigh, had been expelled from the cavern, where all had thought them so securely entrenched, and now it was that our friends received another striking proof of Zero's intense cunning, and of the absolutely perfect knowledge which the man possessed regarding the mountain fastnesses in the immediate neighbourhood of his quarters.

Foolishly enough, the little band had failed to notice the singular fact that the air in the cave was at all times fresh and crisp, instead of being extremely heavy and "muggy," as is ordinarily the case in long, unventilated caverns; and it was only now that they realised the truth, which was that Muzi Zimba's home was situated in the very heart of an immense volcano, which had been extinct for ages, but whose final convulsions had probably torn the range in two, and formed the kloof, or pass, of the Dark Spirit of Evil.

This fact, however, was perfectly well-known to their astute and unscrupulous foe, and, appreciating his knowledge at its right strategic value, and sending on by night a large party provided with an immense rope-ladder, Zero had occupied the adjacent heights above and in the rear of Leigh's position, and had actually dropped three hundred men down through the very crater of the extinct volcano; and the first intimation which the defenders of the cave had received of the presence of this large force in their immediate rear, came to them in the objectionable form of a well-aimed volley poured into their very backs at point-blank range, just at the moment of the delivery, by Zero with his main army, of a furious attack upon their defences in the mouth of the cave.

To turn their attention to the force ambushed in their rear would, of course, have been to let the slaver-chief in upon them, when the cavern would have literally become a shambles, and every man of the party would have died a dog's death, for the ambushed foe was securely entrenched between the position of our friends and the entrance of the mountain burrow leading to the old well.

Choosing the least of two evils, Leigh drew his men together, and then launched them like a thunderbolt down the hill and into the very heart of Zero's force, which they drove before them like chaff before the wind. Then, getting right through the ranks of the slavers, our friends, to the utter bewilderment of the foe, ignored altogether the cover of the forest, and commenced to fall back steadily upon Equatoria, in order, of course, to effect a junction with Grenville and Kenyon, whom Zero, perhaps naturally, imagined to be lying dead in the cavern along with poor Ewan and upwards of a score of the Atagbondo, who had fallen victims to the first treacherous and fatal discharge of the ambushed foe.

In the running fight which had ensued, the loss on the side of our friends had not been worth speaking of, whilst Leigh, with his repeater charged with explosive bullets, had dropped an enemy on every hundred yards of ground from the mountain to the skull-shaped knoll. But when the slavers once sighted the mighty volumes of smoke ascending from their burning town, they naturally scented something extremely wrong, and Zero's active mind instantly jumped to the likeliest solution of the mystery, and told him that Grenville and the great Zulu, both of whom he hated beyond expression, were revenging themselves upon his force at home, and stamping out his town.

This caused the slaver to throw the whole of his available force, at any cost, upon the desperate little band, and drive them in upon the town pell-mell, with fearful loss upon both sides, for the Atagbondo had contested every inch of ground, with a stubborn valour little short of incredible when it is borne in mind that to rifle, spear, and axe, they could only oppose their rough-hewn wooden clubs.

Of the Zanzibari carriers nothing had been seen since the very commencement of the fight, for they had been placed for safety in the hindmost cavern of all, as being worse than useless to the fighting brigade; but whether the cowards were still in hiding there, or whether the ambushed slavers had found and massacred the wretched men forthwith, was, of course, as yet unknown, though, as the slavers in the cavern had followed our friends out when they fled the spot, it was more than probable that the fellows were still where their masters had left them.

Seeing, however, that the Mormon leader was almost certain to have their old location searched for the baggage and belongings of the party, Grenville thought it much better to make a virtue of necessity, and to communicate the position of affairs to the old man without further delay, adding that, on the whole, he almost thought he would prefer to let even the Mormons divide the goods and chattels of his friends, rather than see them calmly appropriated by such a wretched craven crew.

Our friend accordingly asked an audience of the aged Prophet--for by this high-sounding, but somewhat empty, title the old man was designated by his own people--and informed him that in the old hermit's cave upon the northern mountains there lay very much valuable baggage and ammunition, which, unless it was instantly looked after, would probably be opened and appropriated by the thievish bearers, and he added that it would be quite unnecessary to send an armed force to take possession, as the wretched cowards would run away at the first sight of an armed man.

The prophet briefly acknowledged the information, and then dismissed Grenville, first, however, promising that the little party should have the use of their own well-stocked medicine-chest immediately upon its arrival in Equatoria--a favour which Kenyon had most earnestly impressed upon our friend the absolute necessity of inducing the Mormon to grant, if by any means in his power he could prevail upon him to do so.

Just before nightfall the Zanzibaris made their unwilling appearance, bearing their master's baggage, and being driven along, like sheep for the slaughter, by a couple of formidable-looking and heavily-armed Mormons, and the whole property of the little band was at once deposited in the public hall, with the exception of the much-desired medicine-chest, which was delivered, without loss of time, to the waiting Kenyon, who particularly required its contents for immediate use in poor Leigh's case, the complications of which were already causing this amateur doctor much mental worry and very grave anxiety, as the patient after becoming conscious for a few moments, had again relapsed into a state of complete coma.

That night all slept an uneasy, troubled sleep, for the common hall was packed to suffocation with men, women, and children; and as almost all the late combatants were more or less wounded--many very severely so-- the building was more like a hospital than anything else, and no one was particularly sorry when the great doors were opened in the morning, and an announcement was made by the officer on guard that all must leave the place to obtain food, and that the Holy Three would sit in judgment upon the prisoners at high noon that very day.

This judgment was a very impressive affair, and was held in the public hall. In two long lines sat the combatants of the previous day, facing one another on opposite sides of a square, and all closely guarded by the Mormon host. At the head of the room sat the Ancient Prophet, supported by two other very venerable-looking men--these three being the accredited representatives in Africa of the Mormon Holy Three--whilst at the lower end of the square, huddled together like frightened sheep, were the women and children of Equatoria, who knew not what to expect from the stern judges, whose iron code of laws was, they were well aware, as unchanging as the laws of the Medes and Persians.

Kenyon, who was, of course, by profession, a physiognomist, completely forgot all his own personal danger in the absorbing interest which he took in the varied and changing expressions of the anxious faces which surrounded him on every hand.

The fallen and discomfited slavers looked what they were--partly sullen, partly indifferent, and wholly despairing, for well they knew that no mercy could be expected at the hands of the tribunal into whose clutches they had fallen; Zero, utterly mad with rage, and sulky as a bear; whilst it almost made the beholder laugh to notice the striking faces of Amaxosa the Zulu, and Barad, the Chieftain of the Stick. The eyes of these men were positively like coals of fire, and were absolutely riveted on the hated countenance of the slaver-chief, who seemed almost uneasy under the burning intensity of their threatening gaze.

Grenville, chivalrous as ever, was busily endeavouring to infuse hope and comfort into the heart of poor Lady Drelincourt, who was the only person in the assembly allowed to sit in the presence of the judges.

When perfect silence had been obtained, the old Prophet rose to his feet and commenced a direct and startling indictment of Zero and his band of ruffians, who had, he said, robbed and pillaged the fraternity of the Elect in the most impudent and bare-faced manner, and had, moreover, murdered out of hand a number of messengers, who had been sent to them with positive instructions from head-quarters, to return at once to Salt Lake City, report themselves without delay to the Holy Mormon Trinity, and render a full account of their stewardship; and in consequence of Zero's disregarding these definite and repeated commands, the Prophet had, he explained, been sent out with a very great array of the Saints by the Three Unsleeping Ones, who watched over the welfare of the one true faith, and whose written instructions he carried with him, to demolish the stronghold of these audacious rebels, and to execute fully retributive justice upon these men of sin, whose evil and wicked doings had come up, with very evil savour, into the nostrils of the Holy Ones who dwelt across the seas, whilst in Africa he had himself found that, owing to the outrageous conduct of these reprobates, the very name of Mormonism had become a by-word for all that was

100

wholly and irredeemably bad.

The Prophet then brought forward a number of witnesses to prove unauthorised deeds of violence and of blood against Zero and his band, all being without exception classed in the one dreadful category, and the testimony of one of these not only proved the slaver-chief to have been guilty of countless murders in Africa, but deposed that, in the speaker's own un-regenerate days, he had himself been an eye-witness of the shooting of Mr. Harmsworth in New York-- this diabolical and cold-blooded murder having, as Kenyon had opined, been committed by the hand of Zero, in revenge for what he considered to be a personal slight.

The aged Prophet then consulted briefly with the two elders who were his co-representatives in Africa of the Mormon Trinity, and, once again rising to his feet, briefly and clearly pronounced sentence of death.

The whole of the renegade band would die by the rifle at sundown that very night, and their carcases would be thrown to the wild beasts of prey, whilst Zero himself would be crucified at noon on the following day, and his body would be left to the vultures and the crows.

The sentence was evidently what all had foreseen; for, with the exception of a very few despairing shrieks from the women, there was neither voice nor sound.

The old Mormon concluded his harangue by saying that the women and children would be conveyed by his men to the nearest seaport town, and their passage paid to any civilised country they desired to reach, after which the Brotherhood of the Saints entirely washed their hands of them. For a brief instant one could have heard a pin drop, then from the poor creatures at the bottom of that living square there went up one mighty gasp of intense relief, followed by a babel of blessings upon their ancient judge, from which it was quite clear that the poor wretches, who were, most of them, more sinned against than sinning, had fully expected to find themselves and their little ones devoted to the same red grave as their wicked lords and masters.

As the old Prophet ceased speaking, Kenyon suddenly started to his feet, holding up his hand to attract the attention of the judges, and when silence again reigned supreme, and when every eye in that vast assemblage was curiously fixed upon him, quietly but clearly, he spoke out.

"Sir," he said, "I know, and fully admit, your powers of judgment here, by the right of might; but you also are an American, as I am, and I, therefore, ask that, in courtesy to the Stars and Stripes, you will even yield to my prior claim upon the body of this scoundrel, Zero, and allow the executioner of the States, to end his sinful life."

"Who art thou, and whence knowest thou me?" queried the astonished Mormon.

"I, sir," was the cool reply, "am Stanforth Kenyon, of the New York Detective Force, and I have followed this fellow hither from the New World, just as you have done, and, having been the first to find him, I, therefore, think my claim the best, and my case, the Harmsworth murder, on American ground, being now indubitably proved by your own witness, this Zero can no longer now escape the law."

"By repute, I know you well, Detective Kenyon," came the answer, "but Uncle Sam, for once, goes empty-handed. The Elect, as you very well know, recognise no law outside themselves, and allow no interference with their affairs, on the part of the unbelieving and accursed Gentiles. Nay," as Kenyon attempted to speak again, "I cannot hear you further. I sit here, with my colleagues, as the representatives of the heaven-taught Holy Three, and what I have said I have said."

Then, after another short conference with his fellows, the old Mormon announced that the business of the meeting was now concluded, and that his decision with regard to the disposal of the remaining prisoners would be announced at noon next day.

All were at once returned to their prison in the common hall, with the exception of the wretched slavers, who, to the number of nearly three hundred, were immediately led out to execution, and were shot, like mad dogs, in accordance with the unchanging decree of the Mormon Holy Three, whilst Zero, heavily ironed, was forthwith consigned to the condemned cell in the public building, knowing that he must, in a few hours, suffer the extreme agonies of the awful death by torture, which he had himself often and often inflicted upon his helpless and unresisting fellow-creatures.

Chapter 18: A Friend in Need

That very night, when our friends were conversing together in the house of their prison, a guard appeared with a small note, which he handed to Kenyon, and signified that he was to await his answer.

At once tearing open the cover, the wonder-stricken detective read the simple message:--

"Follow the bearer.

"Weston Abbott (`Noughts and Crosses')."

Springing to his feet in joyful haste, he quietly whispered to Grenville, "A friend at court! by Jove, old man! The note is from Uncle Sam's own trusted correspondent in Salt Lake City. We're in luck again," and, indicating to the officer his willingness to comply with the instructions contained in the note, Kenyon quickly followed the man out of the hall.

To the astonishment of our friend, the fellow led him directly to the ancient Prophet's room, where he found the old man very comfortably domiciled, and prepared to receive him most kindly, though still in a strictly business-like manner.

"Well, Mr. Kenyon," he said, "so in this out-of-the-way part of the world we meet at last, and I assure you that it gives me pleasure to know you personally. I am the man who wrote this note, and am also your regular and constant correspondent in Salt Lake City.

"Now, I want you just to tell me the whole history of this affair, and why I find you here at the ends of the earth, when I thought you in New York. Tell me all; for, I assure you, we are at our wits' end to know how to deal with these English people, whom, particularly the woman and child, I rather shrink from slaying."

Kenyon then gave him a full, true, and particular account of the whole expedition, adding that the presence of Lady Drelincourt in Equatoria was still an enigma to him, as he believed her dead in England, slain by Zero's hand; but that the poor woman was still so weak and hysterical that they had not liked to question her, especially whilst her recovered husband hung between life and death. The detective also touched warily upon the destruction of East Utah by

103

Grenville and his friends some years before, palliating their conduct there, by pointing out how very necessary it had seemed to them to rescue Miss Winfield and her father from their captors. To Kenyon's surprise, however, the old Mormon frankly told him that Grenville had in this case, also, only anticipated the intentions of the Holy Three in Utah itself, where they had absolutely enrolled an army of the Saints to eat up the whole of this rebellious African community as soon as they could find out the precise whereabouts of East Utah-- a task which had, however, proved too difficult for them; and Zero's idea had been to found a colony of his own, supported by the abominable traffic in slaves, and, by drawing into it (under the name of Mormonism) all the cut-throats and scoundrels he could lay hands on, to make the community much too strong for even the Saints to overcome him or prevail against him, and eventually no doubt, by exercising the power of the enormous wealth which he had wrung from suffering flesh and blood, to usurp the supreme authority in Salt Lake City itself.

Far into the night this curious pair sat talking of matters vitally interesting to both, and though the old Prophet would not absolutely commit himself to any promise regarding Kenyon's friends, he willingly undertook to do his best for them, adding that, so far as he was concerned, he rather liked them all, and should be glad to do the detective a good turn by setting them all free, but that there were many matters of policy to be considered by himself and his colleagues ere they could see their way to any definite decision upon this head.

In the morning, when Grenville and Kenyon were released from the room which they had been allotted, next to that occupied by the still unconscious Leigh and his anxious wife and child, they were surprised to notice the unusual quiet which overhung the place, but soon found that one of the old Mormon's earliest measures of policy had consisted in starting off to the southward the whole of the female population of Equatoria at dawn, accompanied by their children, and convoyed by five hundred of his own well-armed band.

Immediately breakfast was over, every soul remaining in the town was summoned to another grand assembly, at which it was formally announced, to the astonishment and annoyance of everyone, that Zero had succeeded in filing through his fetters, and had decamped in the night, together with the Zulu Amaxosa and the Chieftain of the Stick, and, therefore, said the stern judges, when these men were recaptured, all three would be crucified without mercy, and Zero, for this additional offence, would be nailed head-downwards to the awful cross .

The prophet then proceeded to say that, after due and careful consideration of the whole peculiar circumstances of the case, the Holy Three had decided to give life and unconditional freedom to all the rest of the prisoners, both white and black, and to present them in addition with large and handsome rewards for the way in which they had acted, as there could be no doubt that the fearful slaughter inflicted by the English party upon the rebel crew, had alone saved the Mormon community from having to fight several severe battles, from losing very many lives of valued men, and perhaps, owing to their lack of knowledge of the district, failing, after all, to accomplish their desired object. For the gentle English lady, and for the injured "People of the Stick," the Holy Three had nothing but sympathy, and had, therefore, decided to apportion the immense spoil taken from Zero--amounting to nearly a million of money--into three equal parts: one for the Mormon community, one for the Atagbondo--to enable them to rebuild their kraals, to buy new wives and weapons, and stock their enclosures with oxen and with goats--and the third share for the English-Zulu party, who had behaved so well and fought so grandly, and amongst whom was classed Detective Kenyon of Uncle Sam's police.

It was a bold course to take, and the old Mormon had unquestionably done a wise thing when he weeded out, and started on the home journey in charge of the women and children of Equatoria, all the possible malcontents of his own band. Still, the Mormons had already seen such a lot of bloodshed that they probably thought the course adopted by their leaders to be the wisest; at all events, they raised no voice against it.

The aged Prophet had, as he afterwards confided to Kenyon, positively no other course open to him under his instructions: either he must declare the party guilty, and cut them off, one and all, absolutely without exception; or he must liberate them unconditionally, congratulate them upon the success of their actions, and give them large rewards for the valuable services they had rendered to the community in destroying the slavers; and this latter course the old gentleman had, fortunately, seen his way to take.

The old fellow would, however, listen to no word of pleading or of explanation for either Amaxosa or Barad, and frankly said that he dared not leave the country until Zero was known to be actually dead, as otherwise he would himself get into very serious trouble at head-quarters, and experience an unpleasantly warm time of it on his return; and he accepted with grateful alacrity Kenyon's offer to assist with his own party in the search for the missing man--an offer which Grenville gladly concurred in, saying that none of them could know a moment's perfect rest until this slippery villain was finally disposed of.

To our friends, the unexplained absence of Amaxosa and of the Chieftain of the Stick was, of course, a complete enigma. Only of this one thing were they sure: that, though both might have either followed or have preceded the slaver-chief--probably the former--they certainly had not escaped along with him, but would, on the contrary, never rest until the rascal's life-blood had washed their spears and clubs.

Chapter 19: A Forced March

After arranging with the old Mormon to start out with Grenville and a scouting party of Zulus at dawn of day, Kenyon turned into the room jointly occupied by himself and Grenville; but, both being overwrought by the events of the day, entirely failed to find the sleep they sought, and finally rose and strolled outside for a moonlight smoke, carefully taking with them their restored and treasured rifles. Both felt relatively happy, for the fear of death--and, however brave a man may be, a violent death is still a fearsome thing--the fear of death, I say, no longer weighed upon them; and the fact that Leigh had that night taken a favourable turn, which placed him out of danger, had also lifted a load of sorrow from the heart of each; and as they strolled quietly along, the pair talked pleasantly of home and friends, and of an early start for England.

Just as the twain reached the limits of their stroll, and were about to turn back and have another try to sleep, Grenville's keen eye detected a movement in the long grass at his right hand. Throwing forward his rifle, he was about to fire, when a shrill, peculiar whistle broke upon the night air, and, dropping the butt of his rifle upon the ground, he stood expectant, whilst Amaxosa coolly stalked forth from his lair, and, advancing to where they stood, gravely saluted them.

"Greeting, Inkoosis, greeting," said the great Zulu; "it does my heart good to see ye free again, and gun in hand. And now, my brothers, lead me, I pray ye, to the ancient man of this people of many women and three kings, for I have news to tell him--news which will not wait; and ye must be my mouth to him, O chiefs!"

"My brother," answered Grenville, laying a hand kindly on the shoulder of his stalwart friend, "knowest thou that, because of thy departure, he has sentenced thee to death; ay, thee, and Barad the Hailstorm with thee."

"Nay, my father," replied the Zulu, "I knew it not, nor do I care whether I live or die; yet do I think the ancient one will gladly hear my words."

Quickly returning to the public hall, Kenyon sent in word to the old Prophet that the Zulu chief had returned of his own accord, and had news of much importance for his private ear.

A few minutes elapsed, and then all were ushered into the united presence of the Holy Three, where, utterly disregarding the frowning looks cast upon him, the great Zulu thus commenced his stirring tale:--

"Hear my words, O ye ancient ones, and let the message of the child of the Zulu sink down into your ears; for his words are heavy words to hear, yet come they from a straight and friendly tongue."

Then addressing himself to Grenville, "Yesternight, my father," he began, speaking rapidly and forcibly in Zulu--"yesternight I had it in my mind that Zero, the Black One, would escape and break his bonds, and in the same mind was also the Chieftain of the Stick; he knew no speech of mine, nor knew I aught of his, my father, yet eye looked into eye, and each knew well the secret thought of each.

"We soon slipped past the sleepy guards and out into the night, but naught had we in our hands, my father, and so we left behind the ruined kraals, and hid us in the bushes by the well.

"Long did we wait, but yet we had no doubt, and, so when half the night was gone, there came to us the ghost of him, the ancient one, who dwells in yon lonely grave upon the northern hills--alas! my father, that I let him pass me by, but empty hands are evil things wherewith to face a well-armed spook, and in his grasp he swung a mighty axe, dripping with human blood.

"And so we waited, and when the Father of the Spooks had left us half-an-hour, then my thought changed, and I knew it was no spook that passed us by, but the black one, Zero himself, escaped in Muzi Zimba's dress, and so I beckoned to Barad, my father, and down the well we went to follow on his trail; but when we reached the narrow mountain pass, we found it all blocked up with mighty rocks rolled from above, so that we could not move them. Then climbed we forth again, and, skirting round the mountain, we filled our ready hands with arms from the dead who lie out yonder; and so sped we onwards through the night running our utmost speed, but naught did we see, my father, until at dawn we struck the Black One's footsteps crossing the western veldt, and these we followed till the sun grew hot at noon, and so we tracked him to the thorn-girt kraal of a mighty host of low black fellows; those men, they were, my father, whose king was here when first we hither came.

"Lying hid, O chief, we watched, as well we might, and when the sun went down, the host set out, led forward by the Black One, and the track they took, my father, was the track of the women and the children who have gone towards the sea.

"And then, my father, did I leave the Chieftain of the Stick to mark the trail, and follow on their rear, whilst I returned at speed to tell thee all.

"And now, O chiefs, think wisely and think quickly what ye do. There is no time to waste--your army, split in twain by thrice a thousand men, must travel like the wind if ye would happen on the spot, ere Zero eats your friends and stamps them flat."

Briefly and succinctly, Grenville gave the Mormons the substance of the Zulu's thrilling news, adding that, from his own knowledge, he could tell them that this king was a very great warrior and the most notorious slave-dealer in all the country side, with a fighting band of quite three thousand men, who were experts in the use of both bow and spear.

Replying, the old Prophet said that he and his colleagues freely pardoned the Zulu and his sable friend, and also thanked them for their zeal, and would now ask further what course Grenville, who knew the country so well, would advise them all to follow. Knowing, however, that Amaxosa must have fully thought out his plan of action, Grenville informed him that the ancient ones had pardoned his escape, and that of Barad, and would wish to hear his plan for eating up the foe.

The great Zulu had quietly sat him down, and taken snuff to his heart's content, but now he rose to his feet, and drawing himself up to his full height, addressed himself to Grenville.

"O my father," said he, "think ye these people here can fight, think ye that they can travel on a long, weary road? For thus shall the matter go:--Seest thou, my father, that yonder comes the dawn. At dawn, next day but one, will the evil Black One, backed by all his wicked host, fall on the white men as they sleep close by the burning mountain; and it shall be, my father, that while the Black One sets a snare for the white men, we ourselves will set a snare for him. Thus, when he rises to fire upon our friends, will we fire on him and his, and take him by surprise. Then will our friends upon the mountain wake and shoot their shots. So shall the Black One find himself between two heavy fires. But think upon the weary way, my father, for much I doubt that few will win it, and therein lies my fear; for, spread out wide upon the veldt and weakened, Zero will eat us up, and stamp us flat for ever. Well, even so, my father, we can but try, and if we die 'twill be a brave man's death, facing a savage foe."

Grenville detailed the whole scheme to the Mormons, urging its adoption without a moment's delay, in view of the tremendous journey--quite a hundred English miles--which must be accomplished at high pressure if they would save the first detachment, and, indeed, themselves; for, if Zero once disposed of half their army, with the enormous force at his back, he would very soon render an account of the remainder.

Our friend recommended that the entire band should start at once, and push on at top speed until the sun was too hot to allow of further progress; then, after resting in the heat of the day--the moon being, fortunately, at the full--they must go for their lives throughout the summer night, until the advent of the sun again drove them from the road, resuming their journey with the cool of evening, and so go ever forward, and hope to be in time. Clearly, there was nothing else for it, and the Mormons rapidly assented to the plan, and all filed out of the room, leaving the Zulu where he sat, for exhausted nature had asserted her rights, and the man was fast asleep.

The Mormon force could not leave the place under an hour, and from long experience of the ways of these active children of the veldt, Grenville well knew that that precious hour would give back to the great Zulu all his magnificent powers, and enable him to lead the party until noon, faster than most of them would care to go.

The sun was already high in the heavens by the time that Grenville and Kenyon had succeeded in getting the Mormons under weigh, and their own breakfast being then ready, Grenville waked Amaxosa, and all three partook of a hearty meal, feeling quite sure that they would soon overtake the main body.

Leigh, with his wife and child, all the wounded, and a guard, which consisted of the few remaining "People of the Stick," were left behind in Equatoria, there being no other course open to our friends, as it was obviously impossible to carry the sick and wounded with them on a forced march, and probably into the very teeth of a desperate and extremely doubtful battle.

Grenville, however, took two carrier pigeons with him, telling Dora that if the fight was going against their party he would send her word by one of these, when she must depart at once from Equatoria with her party, cross the chasm by means of the traversing cage, must cut the rope behind her, and by causing her men to again turn the course of the mountain stream into the northern marsh, lay bare the rocky pathway down the kloof.

When her party reached the veldt it would at once strike out due east and travel night and day until some of the wandering Arab slavers were met with, when Grenville considered it likely that the promise of large rewards would induce these men to afford her safe escort to some seaport town. The plan did not, of course, promise particularly well; but, on the other hand, it was infinitely better than sitting still and waiting for Zero to return and torture everyone to death, and Grenville well knew that the gallant "warriors of the Stick" would fight for "their sister," if need arose, as long as they had a leg left to stand on.

And so the trio bade farewell to the tearful Dora, begging her to be of good comfort, as if they could but arrive in time there would be little fear of the result; and so they passed away and left her once again, alone in this hated Mormon town--yet not alone, for she had now her husband and her child, and these two needed all her loving care.

Chapter 20: The Hand of God

As our friends had anticipated, they found little difficulty in overtaking the Mormon crowd, and, at once going to the front, they set the rescue-party a very different pace to that hitherto travelled by them, and keeping them at the work, despite their murmurs and protests, had knocked off fully twenty miles by noon, and at four o'clock insisted upon a fresh start being made, keeping the pace easier, however, until evening came on.

The three aged Mormons were carried by the Zanzibaris in hammocks, so that these formed no obstacle whatever to their forced marching.

Soon the moon came up in all her radiant loveliness, casting a weird and silvery glamour over the wide expanse of veldt on every side, and on the distant horizon there ever hung the blazing, star-like cone of the distant mountain-peak, for which the leaders steered. And so forward through the livelong night they pressed, faint yet pursuing, and when at dawn of day all crept into cover, and threw their wearied bodies on the ground, Amaxosa, who had been acting as whipper-in, brought up to the front the glad news that only twenty men had so far fallen by the way.

The mountain was distant now but twenty miles, and all felt relatively happy, for it was a shrewd count that three thousand naked savages, even though led by Zero, would not make very much of a figure when they found themselves between two bands, each of five hundred desperate whites, armed for the most part, with quick-firing rifles.

Grenville, Kenyon, and Amaxosa had watched and slept by turns, the last watch before night being the Zulu's, and when his friends woke up they found the chief excessively uneasy in his mind regarding the weather, which looked to him like storm.

However, the party set out as soon as the moon began to rise, and had arrived within a mile of the mountain, and had despatched the great Zulu on ahead to scout, before the storm broke upon them.

The heavens by this time were transformed into an enormous mass of dense, black, lowering clouds, which had sunk until they almost shrouded the waning moon herself, which as yet, however, sailed along in a narrow glorious belt of glittering azure, looking far more lovely from contrast with the frowning bank of clouds which hung above her, and which stretched away in every direction ominous in their sullen death-like quietude.

The Zulu had not left the main body above five minutes when the inky-looking vault right over head was suddenly rent in twain as if some giant hand had ripped the veil of clouds, and heaven and earth seemed fairly to meet for one brief instant in a dazzling, blazing glare of lurid light, which flooded veldt and mountain, rock and river, for miles around the spot, and was instantly succeeded by an unremitting roll of thunder, which seemed to shake all nature to her utmost depths, and threaten earth with chaos worse confounded.

Hardly had the mighty echoes died away than the report of firearms could be heard, in scattered shots, away under the mountain side. The reason was evident: the Mormons had been on the alert, and the terrific blaze of lightning had, no doubt, revealed to their watchful sentinels, the ambush of the hidden savage foe. Sure enough, next minute there came the steady rolling echoes as the Winchesters opened fire in ringing volleys, upon the mass of men before them.

Speeding across the veldt, Grenville and his band endeavoured to take up a flank position where they would run no danger from the bullets of their friends, and, aided by another blazing flash, were almost within range of Zero's troops, which were represented by a dark moving mass upon the veldt, when suddenly and without an instant's warning, a most awful thing happened.

The moon was waning fast and the light was growing dim, when the countryside for miles and miles was all at once illuminated with a brightness vivid as the glory of the noonday sun himself. This was no passing flash of lightning; but there, right above the blazing peak itself, hung a mighty zone of dazzling, blinding fire; for one brief instant thus it stayed, then, with a mighty roar, which rent the earth and quaked the giant rocks, and dwarfed out of recognition the thunders of the sky, the volcano all at once blew up, driving its shattered fragments to the winds of heaven.

Almost at Grenville's feet the earth yawned wildly, and where one moment before had been lovely veldt and sparkling river, there appeared only a mighty chasm, from whose abysmal depths rose fearsome sounds and pungent scalding vapours.

For an instant, all was inky blackness and the quietude of death; then, the storm-clouds driven wildly in every direction by the might of the explosion, the moon shone out once more, and revealed an awful sight.

113

The mountain-peak was gone--gone, forever, its fragments scattered wide across the veldt, whilst between the foot of the mountain and the position of our friends lay a gulf two hundred feet across, unbroken, save by a tiny island of rock--measuring, perhaps, twenty square yards-- which still stood in its very centre. All round the rock--and, perhaps, a hundred feet from its upper edge-- there washed a sea of boiling, bubbling water, lashed to frenzy, and heated red-hot, by the streams of burning lava which, all the time poured themselves into the chasm. In every direction this yawning abyss spread itself out, far as the eye could see, and the effect of its presence was to practically divide the land in two.

Of the Mormons who had held the mountain, and of their savage native foes, not a vestige could be seen. The earth had simply opened her mouth upon them, and down alive into the pit had gone thousands of men, women, and children, both white and black, young and old, friend and foe, consigned, in one dread prayerless instant, to an eternal stygian grave.

But stop! The moonlight grows, the light increases as the clouds clear off. And what moves on yonder pinnacle of rock? Two human forms, they seem-- they are. And now, 'fore God, see how they fight--fight wildly, furiously, for life! Life! Life on such an awful place as this! Better, far better, certain sudden death!

One moment Grenville watched, then springing to his feet, he sent a wild cry of encouragement across the chasm; and in proud and instant answer, pealing across the vast abyss, and waking every sleeping echo in the mighty rocks, came the defiant Zulu war-song, and in one moment more, every child of the Undi within that band was on his feet, ranging up and down the chasm's edge, shouting the war-cry of his famous chief, and seeking means to aid him.

Little help did the Lion of the Zulu require from mortal hands; unarmed he was, but, dashing upon his single foe, he dexterously avoided a swinging blow from the ready axe, and seized him by the throat. Down went the pair, and over and over they rolled, fighting the while like cats, whilst our friends watched, with parted lips and straining, eager gaze, expecting each instant that both combatants would shoot into the abyss of fire beneath. All at once the struggle ceased, for the Zulu had dashed his opponent's head upon the rocks and stunned him. Springing to his feet he sent a cry of victory pealing across the chasm; there was an upward whirl of the foeman's shining axe, and next instant, with a mighty effort, he cast a bleeding human head across the space between.

The ghastly trophy fell at Grenville's feet, and the head was the head of Zero, the slaver-fiend. Then lifting in his powerful arms the headless trunk, the Zulu cast it into the wild abyss beneath his feet, and thus revenged himself for all the wrongs suffered by his proud spirit, and all the tears and blood of countless slaves, both black and white, shed by this curse of Equatorial Africa.

The victory was complete, and their object was accomplished, yet all forgot it in the awful gloom of the moment, cast heavily upon them by the recollection that they stood upon the graves of thousands, who but a few moments ago had walked the world in health and life--thousands brought to a swift and awful end in one brief instant of time; and each man felt that the hand which slew them was the hand of God.

Clearly, however, something must be done to relieve Amaxosa; for he shouted to them that the rock was fast becoming red-hot, and would shortly scorch his feet beyond endurance.

Fortunately the party had brought Leigh's rocket apparatus with them, and soon succeeded in firing a line across the rock, and hauling upon this, the Zulu quickly received a one-inch rope, which he fastened to the rock by driving Zero's axe firmly into a crevice, and attaching the rope to its haft, and then, the line being drawn taut, hung fearlessly by his hands over the literally boiling flood, and coolly commenced to work his way across. When about twenty feet from the edge, where his friends stood ready to welcome him, a shriek of horror went up as the axe gave way, the line slipped, and his giant form was heard to strike with a sickening blow against the face of the cliff.

The anxious watchers held their breath, expecting to hear the final splash as his senseless body plunged into the awful seething horror far below; but Amaxosa had fortunately kept his head, and in spite of the wrench received, and of the fearful blow, he hung on like a leech, and was soon drawn into safety and tended anxiously by friendly hands, and none too soon, for but one pace away from the abyss his senses left him, and he fell prone upon the earth, but was soon brought back again to life and health.

Silently the dawn of another lovely day came gliding over the earth, but our friends saw it not, for all slept a troubled and unhappy sleep until wakened by the fiery sun himself, when they hasted to put some miles between themselves and the site of the abysmal grave below the mountain; Grenville first despatching a pigeon to Equatoria, carrying glad tidings, as follows: "Victory! All well--Zero dead.--

"Dick."

Slowly the party took their journey back, for all were more or less knocked up with the heavy outward march, and it was the evening of the fifth day when, carrying the head of Zero, they reached Equatoria. No amount of persuasion would induce the old Mormon to part with this ghastly trophy, which he declared he would carry back to Salt Lake City to the Holy Three, in order that no doubt might arise as to the successful accomplishment of his mission.

Chapter 21: Lost and Found

The victorious band marched triumphantly into Equatoria as the shades of night were falling; but their joy, alas! was quickly changed to wailing.

Nowhere was there a soul to be seen in or about the town. Leigh was missing, with his wife and child, the Atagbondo guards, and the whole of Zero's plunder divisible amongst the three bands--all, everything was gone.

On carefully searching the public building, however, the whole of the "People of the Stick" were found tightly bound in the condemned cell, which was fastened from outside. The poor creatures were almost dead with thirst and starvation, having been locked up for over four days. They soon, however, revived under friendly treatment, and then, calling up the interpreter, our anxious friends listened to their moving tale.

As a matter of fact, however, these men had very little to tell beyond saying that the very night the main body had left Equatoria they had been visited by an ancient man, the biggest Forest Fetish in those parts, and called by him to a "great dance" in the common hall, which was well lighted by priests holding torches in their hands.

He had delivered a long harangue to the "People of the Stick" regarding the gifts they were to send him from their own country, and after this the unfortunate audience heard no more, their senses gradually leaving them under the subtle influence of the smoke from the torches, which made the air heavy with a curious pungent odour. But though the men could neither move nor exercise the faculties of sight or hearing, each realised that he was being fettered and carried away, whilst he gradually yielded to an overpowering desire to sleep. Naught knew they of the Fetish beyond the fact that his habitation was somewhere in the dense and tangled forest of the east, into whose dark avenues no mortal man dare venture, for they were the home of ghosts and spirits, and the haunts of snakes, and wolves, and many evil things.

It was, of course, too late to make any move that night; so, after roundly cursing the ill-luck which had brought this latest misfortune upon them, the tired wayfarers ate their supper, set a watch, and then lay down to snatch a few hours' rest before the dawn.

The earliest gleam of daylight saw Grenville afoot, and with Kenyon, the Zulus, and a couple of hundred Mormons, he commenced to quarter the forest in every direction. Fearful work this was, for the place was simply a tangled and practically impenetrable jungle, upon which even the axes of the party made little impression. For three whole days did the little band prosecute their arduous search, returning to Equatoria each night utterly worn out with their fruitless and cruel labour.

On the third night, when Grenville, thinking sadly upon the unknown fate of his much-loved cousin, supposed his friend Kenyon to be asleep, to his utter astonishment that worthy suddenly shot up to his feet.

"Gods!" he yelled, fairly trembling with excitement. "Gods! I have it. Dick, what cursed fools we've been--how could those priests have taken bound and stupefied people through these thickets, beyond which our axes cannot carry us. Ten to one in sovereigns, I take you straight to their lair at dawn, old man;" and so he did, never making a single mistake, and a mighty queer place they found it, up amongst the tree-tops.

Entering confidently a great hollow tree which stood about a mile from the town, and on the outskirts of the impenetrable bush, Kenyon triumphantly pointed to a strong rough ladder run up the inside of the giant trunk, and mounting this for near a hundred feet, all found themselves in a fair way to enter the abode of the famous Forest Fetish who dominated the timid natives in those parts, and was had--as is always the case--in even more repute amongst them, on account of his abominable extortions and deeds of violence, than was Muzi Zimba, the Ancient Fetish of the Hills, in consideration of his uniform kindness of soul.

High up upon the interlaced branches of the trees were fastened rough boards, thickly covered with grass matting, and on these, from tree to tree, our adventurers followed for upwards of two miles, a perfectly safe and absolutely silent road, of a uniform width of perhaps five feet, until they penetrated into the sacred presence of the arch-humbug himself. A mighty uproar there was, and a great seizing and brandishing of sacrificial knives and swords, as the first of our friends entered the roomy tree-top, boarded throughout, in which the priests had their semi-aerial domicile. But when these rascals, perhaps thirty or forty in number, saw the whole rescue-party file in, and the grim row of frowning muzzles opening in line with their wretched carcases, the entire band simply flopped down upon their knees, and howled for mercy, the "big man fetish"

118

himself making more noise than anyone.

By great good fortune, poor Leigh, with his wife and child, had been preserved for the occasion of a great fetish dance at next new moon, and were soon found and released, and, as restitution was quickly made of all the plunder stolen from Equatoria, our friends contented themselves with giving the rascals what Kenyon called "a jolly good hiding all round," and then drove them out of the forest altogether, and set fire to their abominable nest, the dry matting making a fine blaze amongst the tree-tops, out of which it scared the monkeys, parrots, and other legitimate denizens in very large numbers. The simple "People of the Stick" were astonished at the discovery made by their white associates; for the poor fetish-ridden creatures of these parts had been almost harried out of their lives by the priests, who were supposed to dwell invisibly under a tree, in whose upper branches, however, was located their real abode. Under this tree, which could be reached only by a bridle-path from the rear of the belt of forest, the miserable negro would devoutly deposit his offering, and when returning upon his way to Equatoria, and passing near the hollow tree, two miles off , he would probably find the gift which, not unfrequently, comprised his little all, thrown contemptuously in his path, whilst hidden voices admonished the terror-stricken wretch to hurry off, and bring a better offering, unless he wished to have his heart torn out of his body. This, of course, was "very big fetish" to such a superstitious people, and they would do almost anything to propitiate the awful Spirit of the Air. Not content with these thievish tricks, however, the priests slew very many men, stole the women, and generally played the "hanky-panky spiritualist" game to their hearts' content.

Before liberating the "big man fetish" himself, Kenyon closely questioned him, through the interpreter, regarding the drug which he had used for the purpose of stupefying the "People of the Stick," and found that the feat was accomplished by steeping torches of fibrous bark in a compound made from bruised herbs, and which closely resembled chloroform in its effect, and of which, he added, he had often made quantities for Zero.

Asked if he knew how Zero used the drug, this man at once fully explained the whole "death," stupefaction, and abduction of Lady Drelincourt and her child--a miserable aboriginal savage thus calmly elucidating a mystery which had proved altogether too much for the wisest doctors and keenest detectives in far-away and enlightened England.

Upon Kenyon, however, expressing the most utter disbelief of his statement,

119

the "Fetish" boldly offered to exhibit the result of the experiment in his own proper person, provided the white men would give him some powder and a gun before they went away; and Kenyon having undertaken to make him happy with a flint-lock and six feet of superior English tower-marked "gas-pipe," the man forthwith proceeded to demonstrate the truth of his curious tale.

First obtaining a small gourd of the drug referred to, he then took from a pouch at his side a beautiful little tame white monkey. Next picking a sharp thorn, he coated the point well with the nameless compound, and, giving the instrument to the monkey, pointed to himself. The little animal cunningly concealed the thorn within its palm, and then offered to shake hands with its master, and this ceremony having been performed, the old man held up his hand and exhibited a small red mark in the palm. He then explained that the properties of the drug were distinctly anaesthetic, and that he could not feel the puncture, which was painlessly made; but he would nevertheless shortly go to sleep for three or four days, and then wake up again, being quite recovered, and none the worse for the experiment.

The drug had no perceptible effect upon the man for several hours, but towards evening he began palpably to get very drowsy, and no power on earth could keep him awake. The suspicious Kenyon, however, was not to be "done," and punched and kicked the old man unmercifully--an operation in which he was most ably seconded by Amaxosa, who beat the "cunning man of the witch-finders black and blue" with the handle of his spear, pausing only now and then to take a pinch of snuff. "Ow! my father," he said at last, throwing down the spear in disgust--"Ow, my father, who can beat the life into a dead dog like this? What is gone is gone forever, and the breath will never come again, so we had best throw this low fellow to the jackals; he is far too cunning to live with men."

Kenyon, however, kept his man safely and watched him keenly; he found that during the continuance of the trance there was no perceptible pulse, nor was there any movement of the heart or respiratory organs; it was, in point of fact, an astonishing case of absolutely suspended animation. Everyone who examined the man insisted that he was an undoubted corpse, and ridiculed the very idea of his returning to life; and, to all appearance, he certainly was stone dead, and even Kenyon began to fear that the old fellow, in his eagerness to vindicate his reputation as a witch-doctor, had overdone the thing and settled himself once for all.

On the fifth night, however, the "fetish man" awoke, sat up, coolly asked for his powder and gun, and got both and a double allowance in exchange for his wonderful secret, which he imparted to the delighted Kenyon.

Lady Drelincourt confirmed all that the man had said. She perfectly remembered the pretty pet monkey, which had been brought round by Zero, who was himself disguised as an organ-grinder, and both she and her child had shaken hands with the little creature, and all the rest, of course, was simple to a man of Zero's capabilities, to whom the work of a resurrectionist was an unconsidered trifle, and whose devilish cunning had rightly calculated that the old family doctor would say anything, or sign anything, to protect his friend from the grisly horrors attendant upon a post-mortem examination.

Of her removal by sea poor Dora knew nothing, and her first recollections were upon a steamer bound for Madagascar, some days out from France; and whenever she began to come out of her trance, Madame Zero would promptly renew the dose, and effectually prevent the poor girl from getting loose or making mischief, whilst she was given out on board as being a delicate lady with an extremely feeble mind.

Zero's original intention had been to hold her for ransom, and apply to Leigh for an enormous sum of money; but his "wife" stopped this, feeling sure that it would bring upon the community the vengeance of the outraged English law.

As soon, however, as the slaver knew of Leigh's arrival in his vicinity, he determined upon the devilish plan of forcing Dora to marry one of his own men, and then promised himself the hellish satisfaction of presenting her to her own husband as the wife of another man, and that man, a Mormon .

Having once disposed of the "fetish palaver," Kenyon became more eager than anyone to turn his face homewards, and two days afterwards the whole party accordingly left Equatoria, and after destroying the Bridge of Rope, firing the public building, and razing to the ground the last stronghold of Zero the slaver, his conquerors steered a straight course for the south-western seaboard.

Chapter 22: Farewell

Months later the whole band reached safely a small Portuguese haven on the south-west coast, in which there lay at anchor the Mormon's own steam-vessel, the Brigham Young, and all going on board of her, the old Prophet, who had now become excellent friends with Grenville and his party, ordered steam to be got up, and, running comfortably down the coast, soon landed our friends at Cape Town to wait for the English mail-boat, whilst he himself, after revictualling his ship, set sail for home with the remnant of his victorious army of the "Elect."

Bitter was the final parting between Grenville and Amaxosa, though the great Zulu to some extent concealed his true feelings under the mask of his accustomed stoicism.

"The light has gone out of my sun, my father," he said; "the storm-clouds are very heavy, and my heart is split in twain. What can the chieftain of the Undi say more? Yet, my father, if aught of evil comes upon thee, then, out of the trackless deserts of the unknown land beyond, call thou aloud for Amaxosa, thy true and only son, and thy faithful war-dog will answer, `Here am I, my father!' and will straightway follow on along the narrow, bloodstained path, even through the darksome shadows of the dead, and into the glorious land of the great hereafter.

"Fare ye well, Inkoosis, wise and mighty chiefs!

"Adieu, my little sister, who from the shadows of the cruel past hast come to bless us!

"And to thee, my father--to thee, with whom the spirit of thy son is bound in the bundle of life here and hereafter, to thee the Lion of the Zulu gives his greeting last and best. Greeting to thee, bravest of the brave!

"Greeting and farewell!"

THE END